SUMMONING SEX DEMONS

BECOMING LUST

EMILIA ROSE

To all the good girls who are going to hell after reading this.

CHAPTER
ONE

IZA

HALLOWEEN NIGHT, Mikayla skipped up our front walkway with her black tutu blowing in the chilly breeze and her bright orange hair bouncing with it. She had way too much energy for someone who looked tired during the entirety of the frat party. "Wanna summon some demons?"

"Micky"—I yawned—"it's late."

"Oh, come on!" she exclaimed, looking between Jada and me. "It's Halloween night, the costume party was shit, and I want to actually be spooked. Plus, it's not even eleven o'clock yet, and it's Saturday tomorrow, so no classes."

"John's dick didn't spook you enough?" Jada giggled.

Mikayla exaggerated an eye roll. "Maybe it would've if I could actually see it."

I shoved my key into the front door lock and jiggled it like I usually did to get it to unlock.

She jumped up and down next to me. "Please! Please! Please! Please!"

"Only for a bit," I said, opening the door. "I have to study."

"Meet in your room in five!" she shouted, already halfway up the stairs to dig through her closet and find the Ouija board that she bought on discount November 1 last year. She loved Halloween with a passion, obsessed over ghosts and ghouls, and had even memorized a plethora of spells from when we visited Salem, Massachusetts, last year.

While I didn't particularly believe in the mystical, I played along with her since she was my bestie of seven years. If she were anyone else, I would've laughed in their face for even suggesting that we play with a Ouija board on Halloween.

And it definitely *wasn't* because it kinda scared me.

Maybe …

What if something *did* happen and we summoned a demon who haunted us for the rest of eternity?! I had to finish college and didn't need to worry about some nasty, creepy creature living in my closet for the rest of the semester.

"I'mma change out of this lingerie fit first," Jada called from her bedroom.

After dumping my purse on my desk, I tore off my devil costume, which I ended up feeling self-conscious in the entire night around all those skinnier sorority girls at the party, and pulled on fuzzy pajama bottoms and a tank top. I was so much more comfortable in my own room.

"Coming in!" Mikayla shouted from outside the door. "Best be naked."

My lips curled into a small smile as the door swung open and she stepped in with a Ouija board resting across her arm. Jada walked in a few minutes later with pimple cream all over her face, her coiled hair tied up in two knots on the top of her head, and a bowl of popcorn.

Don't ask me what kind of sorcery she did to get ready for bed so quickly.

Mikayla shut the door and placed the Ouija board on the fuzzy orange rug in the center of my bedroom, then plopped down onto her stomach in front of it. "What kind of demon do you wanna summon?"

"The ones that leave quickly so we can get off to sleep," Jada hummed, smirking at Mikayla because she *knew* it'd make her angry. "I'm tired as fuck, and I want to decorate for Christmas tomorrow."

"Got it." Mikayla winked. "I'll summon the most annoying one just for you."

I sat beside them and crossed my legs, staring down at the black-painted board with white letters on it. I had only ever seen one of these things in the Halloween discount section at Michaels crafts store, but this one looked ... *different.*

"Are you sure this is a Ouija board?" I asked.

"Of course it is!"

Jada squinted at it, then arched a brow. "It doesn't look—"

"Shush! There's no trying to get out of it now. I've already started the summoning."

Jada snorted. "All you've done is touch it."

"And how do you think summoning works?"

"Do you even know what you're doing?" Jada asked.

Mikayla tossed some orange hair over her shoulder. "Of course I do."

I leaned back on my hands and arched a brow at my best friend, who stared down at the Ouija board with the widest, most *I don't know what the fuck I'm doing* eyes. Then, she poked at it and smiled innocently at us.

"You know, I'm more of a witch-spell kinda girl. I haven't had a chance to use this yet."

"Well, do your witch shit then," Jada said, popping a piece of popcorn into her mouth, as if watching Mikayla was her entertainment.

And I mean, it was kinda silly. But I would never tell Micky that.

While Mikayla began muttering something in Latin, I glanced at Jada and hoped that whatever Mikayla was saying wasn't actually going to summon a demon. I didn't believe in it, but Mikayla did. Hard-core. And with what she was saying ... she might just summon something.

Wind whistled outside, making the back screen door slam against the house repeatedly. I looked through the window across from my bed and chewed on the inside of my cheek as Mikayla's voice turned into a soft whisper of foreign words.

"Come out, come out wherever you are, Mr. Demon," Jada hummed.

"Jada, you know that's not how it works," I said. "He has to—"

Thunder boomed through the bedroom, and I jerked back, heart pounding.

Jada smirked and quickly moved the board to the right. "Scared?"

I cut my gaze to her. "No."

Suddenly, Mikayla's eyes rolled back into her head so we could only see the whites. Jada and I shared a look as lightning flashed across her face.

Then, I leaned closer to Jada and lowered my voice. "What did she drink at the party?"

"Apparently, the good shit."

"I feel a presence," Mikayla murmured.

Jada arched a brow. "Girl, you know there ain't no presence in here, right—"

Before she could finish the sentence, another pop of thunder rattled through the house, and the lights turned out. I clutched Jada's hand, breath hitching. Maybe we really weren't alone. It was Halloween night after all …

Anything could happen.

CHAPTER
TWO

ACAROS

"I'M NOT DOING this shit anymore," Haroos growled through his jagged teeth, slamming into The Lounge—a bar made for demons in the human world. "I've been summoned ten times in the past hour by bratty kids playing with Ouija boards." He collapsed on a stool at the bar and grabbed a drink from the bartender. "I fucking hate Halloween."

"Maybe you should've chosen a kingdom other than Wrath to be a demon in," I said.

That hotheaded bastard stood up and stomped over to me. "I didn't choose Wrath, you piece of shit." He slammed his hands against my shoulders, attempting to send me backward in my booth beside my friends. "You try being summoned for once."

"Humans only want to see ugly monsters on Halloween night," Bazzon said. "Like you."

"We have a hard life too, Haroos," Varoth said.

"It can be *really hard* at times." I chuckled.

Twirling around on his heel, he hurled his glass at the bar. "Not again."

And then a moment later, he disappeared into thin air.

"Ah, another summoning," Bazzon said. "Get him off our asses, huh?"

I gulped back another drink and glanced up at Eros and Dani, the king and queen of Lust, who walked into The Lounge. Eros spotted us and headed over while Dani went to flirt with some succubi at the bar, who she'd undoubtedly bring into a Lust Room tonight while Eros watched.

Lucky bastard.

"Acaros, Bazzon, Varoth." Eros smirked. "You're in luck."

"In luck on Halloween night?" I hummed. "This ought to be good."

"You've been summoned."

"Summoned?" Bazzon repeated. "We're never summoned tonight."

Eros pulled up a portal the size of his hand and held it toward the table, letting us see into a candlelit room with three college-aged girls inside it, sitting around a Ouija board cursed with dark magic —something I hadn't seen in ages. One redhead was whispering things that I doubted she understood the meaning of. Another was dabbing at the cream on her face.

And then ... there she was.

Sitting on the floor in fluffy pajama pants, hair thrown up into a messy, curly bun, and nipples taut against her tank top, she stared at her redheaded friend with wide eyes, the candlelight flickering off her face.

"Who's the hot chick with those fluffy—"

"She's mine," I growled.

I didn't know where it had come from, but the words tumbled out of my mouth, followed by a sheer wall of jealousy, possessiveness. Hell, I didn't know what to call it. But all I knew was that, if they truly had summoned us—sex demons—on Halloween night, then nobody but me was going to touch her.

"You good?" Bazzon asked, arching a brow as they all stared at me.

Usually, I slept around all the time and enjoyed sharing the human women and succubi that I was with. But not tonight.

Eros cleared his throat. "Anyway, Dani wanted to head out there, but—"

"We'll go," I said, already standing.

"Not even going to let me finish my beer?" Varoth asked, throwing his arms up in disappointment.

I snapped my hand around his shoulder and pulled him out of the booth. "No."

The portal expanded from Eros's hand, and I shoved my two buddies through it and followed closely behind. After a moment, we came out on the other end in the shadows of the girls' home on the second-floor fire escape.

"I can't believe our power went out because of this stupid storm," the cream-faced girl complained from inside the room, popping a piece of popcorn into her mouth. "How am I going to decorate for Christmas tomorrow if—"

"It didn't go out because of the storm. It went out because there's someone here," the redhead said, closing her eyes and muttering some more Latin. "I can feel their presence. They're here."

"Wanna fuck with them?" Varoth whispered beside me.

After a few more Latin phrases by the redhead—which definitely *weren't* spells by any means, but more like jumbled little words spoken incoherently—Varoth released a gust of magic wind that drifted through the closed window and blew out their candles.

The pretty one with dark skin screamed. "Stop playin', Jada! Light the candle back up!"

"That wasn't me!" Jada grabbed the lighter and relit the candle. "I swear to God, Iza."

Iza … that was her name, was it?

"If you're there, all powerful spirits, show yourself," the redhead said, really getting into it.

When Bazzon went to step out of the shadows, I yanked him back. "Not yet."

They waited for a moment and then another, and then the redhead threw her arms up. "Fuck!"

"All right"—Jada yawned—"I'm calling it a night."

Lightning struck through the sky, thunder cracking overhead.

"I can't believe this," the redhead snarled, following Jada out of the bedroom and flaring her nostrils. "Three hours of Ouija board and witch curses later, and we can't even communicate with a simple ghost! I know I did everything right. Why won't they come out?!"

Jada tugged on one of her curls and frowned as the redhead slumped her shoulders forward and trudged down the hallway. "Happy Halloween!" Jada teased. "I can't wait to decorate for Christmas tomorrow!"

"Happy Halloween to us," the redhead grumbled from down the hall, then slammed her door.

"She'll get over it," Jada said. "You need help cleaning up?"

"No." Iza smiled. "I'm good."

As Jada disappeared down the hallway, I gestured for Bazzon and Varoth to exit the room. "Follow them." My gaze drifted to those coiled brown curls swooping around her face, glowing in the moonlight. "This one is mine."

CHAPTER
THREE

IZA

ANOTHER ROLL of thunder crashed through the night, I crawled into my bed and underneath my covers, snuggling up with my blankets and shutting my eyes. I waited to hear Mikayla's shouts through the house that this was a sign, that a spirit was trying to communicate with us.

But she didn't say a word.

When I couldn't fall asleep immediately, I opened my eyes, sat up in bed, and leaned over to stare out my window. Light blazed out from Mikayla's bedroom next to mine. The hair stood up on my arms.

Why had ... Why had only my power gone out?

Deciding that it was nothing, that I was just hallucinating, I relaxed back into bed and closed my eyes. Mikayla was just getting inside my head now. We had been at it for hours tonight. I must've started believing it myself.

My floorboard creaked, and I snapped open my eyes.

"Mikayla, if you're trying to scare me, it's not working."

The hell it isn't. I am about to piss myself.

Heart pounding, I glanced at the bedroom door, which was shut.

I shifted my gaze around the room to see the closet door, which I knew I had closed. It was now ajar. My mouth dried.

What is going on?

I scanned the room and found nothing. No one. This was my imagination.

"Stop letting her get inside your head," I whispered to myself, grabbing the blankets and pulling them up to my chin. "There are no such things as ghosts. There are no such things as ghosts. There are no such things as—"

Someone brushed their fingers against my ankle that stuck out from underneath my blankets. I shrieked and sat up in the bed, heart pounding inside my chest. I pressed my back against my wooden headboard and reached for my lamp, hoping to God that it'd turn on.

Nothing.

"Wh-what's going on?" I whispered.

"Relax," a man with the deepest voice purred into my ear, followed by the scent of peppermint.

A shiver ran down my spine. I snapped my head in the direction of the voice. Nobody.

Fingers suddenly slithered around my shoulders, then down my bare arms, pushing the blankets away. Goose bumps rose on my skin, and I felt paralyzed to the spot. Two hands disappeared underneath my shirt, the large knuckles making indents as they traveled up to my breasts.

My nipples hardened, the warmth growing between my legs. When he flicked my nipples with his fingers—which felt more like claws—I threw my head back and moaned. I didn't know why it felt so good—*there's a stranger in my bedroom!*—but I couldn't stop the pleasure from surging through me.

"W-who are you?" I whimpered, watching the indent of his knuckles against my shirt.

Waiting for him to flick my nipples again.

"Innocent little human," he hummed, hands traveling *down* my body to the waistband of my pants. "You don't even realize what you and your friends summoned tonight, do you?" He let out a low chuckle that annihilated me. "*Who* you and your friends summoned tonight."

He dipped his hand between my legs and cupped my wet, throbbing pussy. A set of lips brushed against my collarbone, the man's warm breath fanning my bare neck. Another breathy moan escaped my lips.

Moonlight flooded in through the curtains, illuminating the monster in my bed. Sharp teeth, red-tinted skin, large black horns. I didn't even know if I would scream if I could. My mouth was dry, my pussy *wet.*

A demon who must've been twice my size lay beside me and slipped his large fingers inside my cunt. I reached between my legs and seized his wrist, the pressure quickly building up inside my pussy.

"J-Jada! Mikayla!" I shouted, heart pounding.

"Call for them all you want." He used his free hand to lift my chin so I stared directly into his pitch-black eyes. Inside their reflection, I could see into Jada's and Mikayla's rooms, and I watched as they got fucked and fondled by other large demons too. "They're busy."

"W-what are you going to do with me?" I whispered.

"Everything you desire."

Before I could ask any more questions, he flipped me over so I lay on my stomach.

With his knees on either side of my legs, he pinned my hips to the mattress, leaned over me, and grabbed a fistful of my hair, tugging up on it. "Tell me what you desire."

I opened my mouth to speak, but all I could do was moan when I felt how huge his cock was. He ground it up and down against my ass and between my thin, silky pajama shorts. I curled my toes and whimpered, my ass bucking back against his like I didn't have control of my body anymore. My pussy was sopping wet and aching to be filled.

"What do you desire?" he asked again.

"For you to ruin me."

The only words I could summon out of my throat. *Ruin me.*

Ruin me hard. Fast. Deep. I didn't care.

"Good girl," he cooed into my ear from behind, then released my hair and smacked my ass cheeks hard. "Get up onto all fours. I can't promise that I will be gentle with you. My cock is going to stretch out your tight human cunt like no dick ever has before."

Heat rushed through me. I followed his orders and pushed my ass back until I sat on all fours in front of him, my breasts falling out of my tiny tank top and my pussy juices soaking through my bottoms.

He lifted one of my hands off the bed and forced me to wrap it around his large horn. I arched my back and gripped the ridged edges with my palm. Then, he did it with my other hand.

"Don't let go," he said, sprawling one hand across my chest and ripping off my shirt at the seams.

My tits bounced around, my nipples hardening from the sudden chill. I tightened my grip on his horns and clenched.

Instead of ripping off my shorts with his brute strength, he pulled out his cock and pressed it against my pussy from outside the shorts. He rubbed it back and forth against the silky material, pressing harder and harder against it each time.

I curled my toes, waiting for him to shove himself into me. He rested his hands on my ass, pulling the material apart until the seams stretched, then drew a single claw down the center, creating a small hole in my shorts.

He shoved the head of his cock into the hole. I rocked back further and listened to my shorts tear completely down the center as he slid into me. My walls stretched around him, and a cry of pain escaped my lips. His head wasn't even inside me yet, and it hurt.

Badly.

"Please, go slowly!" I whimpered. "I'm a virgin."

A vicious growl escaped his throat. "Even better."

Trying to distract myself from the pain, I moved my hands up and down the length of his horns. He grunted and continued to push himself into me, the pain slowly subsiding, the faster I stroked his horn.

Another grunt, and he slammed himself balls deep into my pussy.

He peeled one of my hands off his horn and laid it across the enormous bulge inside my stomach that reached to my sternum. After pulling himself out of me and leaving me empty, he slammed himself into me again and filled me up, my stomach bulging so much that it nearly looked like I was pregnant.

My pussy tightened around his huge cock, the pressure building up and up in my core.

"I've never had a human take my cock so deep inside her," he growled, thrusting into my tight cunt. He seized my hips in his large hands and used me for his pleasure. "Devils, you take it so well. So fucking well."

I grabbed both of his horns again and stroked them faster, arching my spine enough so I could look back at him. He slithered out his forked tongue and slipped it into my mouth, curling it around mine.

He gripped my waist tighter, his thumb brushing over the head of his cock near my sternum. "Fuck," he groaned, wrapping his free hand around the base of his cock and balls and shoving himself even deeper into me. "Have to stick my heavy balls into you for good measure."

Another moan escaped my lips as I clenched around him.

"You're filled up with every inch of me," he growled. "Now, you're going to beg."

"P-p-please," I whined, gripping his horns tighter. "I want your cum."

"Tight-cunt virgins like you can never take any incubus's cum," he said. "It's nearly impossible to *not* fill you up past your cervix. Begging for an incubus like me to spray his cum into your hole is comparable to begging to get pregnant."

My pussy tightened even harder around him.

"If that's what you want"—he slammed himself into me over and over and over—"then beg me to put a child inside you."

"P-p-please!" I cried, unable to stop myself from moving my hips with his.

When he pulled out, I pushed my hips back so he wouldn't slip fully out of me. I wanted him buried as deep as he could go when his cum spilled into me. I wanted my belly full with all of his cum, with every last drop of it.

"Please," I pleaded. "Breed me!"

Like a vicious animal, he shook my hands off his horns, flattened me out on the bed, and lifted my hips high as possible into the air, ramming himself into me until I screamed out into the mattress. Wave after wave of pleasure rushed through me, my body trembling like it never had.

Then, he stilled.

More pressure flooded through my pussy, and then, as if he felt the pressure too, he pulled out of me. His cum poured out of my pussy and onto the bed, creating a pool underneath me.

"Next time you summon a sex demon, make sure you know what you're doing," he growled, resting his huge cock on my back as more of his cum leaked out of it. He swooped his fingers into the pool underneath me and slammed them back into my pussy. "Innocent humans like you don't know how much you can truly take."

CHAPTER
FOUR

IZA

OH MY GOD.

I stared at the ceiling, naked and panting. Wind rolled in through the slightly cracked window, and I didn't even know if what I thought had happened last night had actually happened. The demon—that sexy, irresistible demon—had left moments after he was inside me.

Moments after he ruined me.

After closing my eyes and bracing myself, I dipped a hand between my legs and slipped a couple of fingers into my aching cunt. My pussy was drenched—and not just in my wetness, but in something thicker.

Something like … cum.

"Iza! If you don't get your ass out of bed, we're going to be late!" Jada shouted from downstairs.

Cursing to myself, I leaped out of bed and yanked the blankets back to see that I had been lying on a huge stain of blood, mixed with cum. I swallowed hard and glanced toward the door in hopes that Jada or Mikayla wouldn't pop into the room at any second.

What was I going to do?! Had that actually happened last night?

Or was I just imagining it? If I was imagining it, then why the hell was there blood on my sheets and cum pooling inside my pussy? It … it had to have been real.

"Iza!" Jada said again.

"Fuck, I'm coming!" I shouted back.

Once I scrambled through my closet and threw on some comfy clothes and a jacket, I swung my backpack over my shoulder and sprinted out of my bedroom and down the stairs to meet Jada and Mikayla in the kitchen, waiting for me to walk to campus to study.

It was our typical weekend activity—get cream-filled Fervor Crisps at Crimson's Bakery, then study. But unlike usual, neither of them spoke a word to each other when I made it downstairs. They both looked lost in their own worlds.

"Heading to the library?" I asked to confirm.

Who knew what had happened last night? What if they were both possessed and decided to bring me somewhere *else* that wasn't the library at all? I had always been a nonbeliever of spirits or demons, but did stuff like what we had for Mikayla.

Now … I didn't know what to believe.

"Crimson's Bakery first," Jada said.

After nodding, I followed them out of the house and down the sidewalk toward Crimson's Bakery, which was thankfully a few blocks away from our apartment. A gust of wind seared my cheeks, so I pulled my hood up and kept my head down.

Halfway to Crimson's Bakery, nobody had said another word.

"So …" I whispered on our walk to Crimson's Bakery. "Any spirits visit you last night, Micky?"

"No," she said hurriedly, glancing over at Jada and me. "What about you guys?"

Jada let out a chuckle, but it wasn't like her usual taunting ones. "Of course not."

"Yeah, nobody visited me either." That must have been all my imagination.

Once we reached Crimson's Bakery and gave our orders, we walked to the table we always sat at since we'd become roommates.

While Jada and Mikayla sat on one side of the table, I sat facing the window.

"It's past Halloween," Jada hummed, breaking the Fervor Crisp apart on her napkin. "But I was thinking that there isn't any harm in … you know … maybe"—her voice dropped to a whisper—"trying out the Ouija board again."

If I didn't believe in the supernatural, then Jada *definitely* didn't believe in any supernatural stuff. She always scoffed at the idea of Ouija boards and ghosts, Halloween haunted hayrides, and … demons.

But if she wanted to try it again, did that mean that it'd happened to her too?

I perked up at the mere thought of meeting that monster again. "Yeah, me too."

Mikayla stiffened. "I don't think that's a good idea."

"Don't tell us you're scared now," Jada said.

"I'm not scared! I'm just being cautious. You don't want to summon too many—"

Jada playfully rolled her eyes. "Oh, come on."

Through the window, I spotted three handsome men, dressed in buttoned overcoats, heading straight for the entrance of Crimson's Bakery. My eyes widened slightly. The tall and muscular one with the messy black hair looked almost identical to … the guy who had been in my room last night.

I blinked a few times and shook my head, hoping that I was just seeing things.

Or at least being overdramatic.

But the closer they approached the door, the more nerves built in my belly.

"Switch seats with me," I whisper-shouted, shooting out of my seat.

"What?"

Before Jada could say another word, I yanked on her wrist to pull her out of the seat and plopped my ass right where she had been sitting. I shrank down into the seat, trying to hide my face behind the flaps of my jacket.

Mikayla giggled. "What, did you see someone that you hooked up with last night?"

My face burned in embarrassment, and while I'd bet that she was talking about someone at the Halloween party, this was someone I was almost certain I'd hooked up with last night. But I didn't know if it was in my dreams ... or real.

The bell on the door clattered, and a wall of peppermint hit me.

Jada stiffened and swiped some hair into her face. "Fuck."

"You too, Jada?" Mikayla hummed.

"Shut up!" she whisper-yelled back.

Our entire table, even Mikayla, stayed quiet as they walked to the counter and ordered.

Jealousy pooled inside my gut at the pretty pink-haired girl with freckles leaning over the counter to flirt with him. I stared down at my half-eaten Fervor Crisp and hoped they'd just leave after they ordered.

Heat coursed through my body and pooled in between my thighs, my panties soaked at the memory—or dream or whatever it was—of that monster inside me last night. But that monster definitely hadn't been human like this guy was.

He had horns, and Mr. Handsome over there didn't.

From the corner of my eye, I saw the trio grab their baked goods off the counter and turn around to head back out the door and disappear from my life forever. And while that might've been the ideal scenario, instead, they took a seat at the table across from us.

Fuck.

When I dared myself to look back up at Jada, the handsome man behind her had his eyes locked on me. I shifted my gaze from Jada to the man, heart pounding inside my chest and nerves zipping through me.

W-why w-was he staring at me ... like that?

Albeit it had been dark, those were the same eyes that I had seen last night.

I knew that they were.

His lips curled into a small smirk, and suddenly, my pussy was clenching and unclenching almost instinctively, as if it remembered the way he'd felt inside me last night … in my dreams. I clutched on to the chair and pressed my thighs together, making the pressure worse.

I jumped out of my seat. "I'll be right back. I need some air."

"Some air?" Mikayla repeated. "What are you—"

Before she could finish her sentence, I zoomed out the door and walked to the side of the building so I wouldn't be tempted to look through the windows at those dark, almost-black eyes that had burned into my skin from the table over.

What the hell was going on with me?! I had been surrounded by good-looking frat boys last night and didn't give a hell. And now, I was freaking out over some handsome, billionaire-looking, huge-muscled man that I didn't even know!

After rubbing my hands over my face, I shook my head. *Get it together, Iza.*

Last night had all just been a dream. It hadn't happened, no matter how much Jada seemed to remember something happening too. Maybe I had gotten drunker than I thought at the party, or maybe someone had slipped a hallucinogen inside my drink. Did they even have liquid forms of hallucinogens?! Or was that my mind making more shit up—

Peppermint drifted through my nose again, and I stiffened.

"Iza," he purred from behind me. "I had a feeling I'd see you again."

CHAPTER
FIVE

ACAROS

IZA TWIRLED AROUND to face me and craned her head up, eyes widening. "Y-you ..."

I hummed, a small smirk crossing my face, "What about me, Hellcat?"

After a wide range of emotions crossed her face, she shook her head. "Do I know you?"

Leaning against the brick building, I tightened my hand around the brown paper bag filled with Fervor Crisps that I had gotten from the café. Her gaze dropped down to my crossed arms for a moment, and she swallowed hard and shuffled her thighs together. I inhaled the thick scent of her arousal, the feel of her body wrapping around mine last night making me *stiff*.

"Do you?" I asked.

Through the widest brown eyes I had seen, she stared up at me and shook her head again. "No, I'm ... I'm just getting you confused with someone I thought I knew ... *sorta*. I'm ..." She looked away again. "I thought I recognized you." Then, she paused. "Wait, h-how do you know me?"

Instead of answering her—because that'd be a long conversation that I wasn't willing to have with a human I could never have—I stepped closer to her and inhaled the sweet scent of oranges. "Didn't like your Fervor Crisp?"

"Wh-what?" she squeaked.

"Your Fervor Crisp." I nodded toward the building, fingers gliding against the smooth material of the brown paper bag in my hand. "You didn't finish it, so I assume you didn't enjoy it this morning."

"I usually do."

"But not today?"

She looked everywhere but at me. "I was ... distracted."

"These are better," I said, holding out the bag to her.

After staring at it for a couple of moments, she grabbed it from me. She opened up the bag and peered down into it, furrowing her brows. "These are Fervor Crisps from the café. How ... how are they better?"

"They're specially made."

"Specially made how?" she asked, voice almost a whisper.

Smirking, I moved closer to her and pulled a Fervor Crisp from the bag. After breaking it in half, the gooey center beginning to drip out, I placed it at her lips. "Eat."

While staring up at me through her lashes, she parted those full lips that I had imagined wrapped around my cock so many times since last night and took a bite of the Fervor Crisp, some white powder coating her lips.

"Good girl."

She inhaled sharply through her nose and inched her thighs together, nipples hardening.

"How do you like it?" I hummed.

She licked her lips and swallowed, a haze crossing her gaze. "It's really ... really good."

My lips curled into a small smirk. "You take it so willingly."

"Wh-what?"

"You take it so willingly," I repeated.

"I do."

Then, as if she realized what she'd said, her cheeks reddened to the shade of Passion Delights back at The Lounge. She tucked some coiled hair behind her ear. "Sorry, I didn't mean it like that. I ... you see ... I think ..."

I captured her chin in my grasp and swiped my thumb across her lower lip. "When you told me that you were a virgin last night, I almost didn't believe it." I pulled her closer. "You're way too fucking cute."

Cute?! If my friends heard me call a human that, they'd laugh their asses off.

But I couldn't help it.

"Last night," she whispered, pupils dilating. "Last night ... wasn't ... real."

"Tell yourself that all you want, Hellcat."

She swallowed. "What's your name?"

"Acaros."

"Well, Acaros, you ... you don't look the same. And I was ... dreaming. I had to be."

I bit back a chuckle. Because if she had been sleeping, this would've been much easier. If she had been sleeping, it would've been like every other night that I spent in someone's bed, feeding off their wet dreams. If she had been sleeping, I wouldn't feel this connected to her.

"Your friends are going to wonder where you are," I said. "Why don't we go see them?"

"We?" she repeated, glancing at the building.

After drawing her closer, I guided her toward the café. "We."

With my hands fastened on her wide hips, she scurried back into the coffee shop and nervously glanced at her friends. But she didn't know that, as long as my fingers were against her body, her friends wouldn't be able to see us.

It was only a power that incubi and some succubi had.

And for some humans, the thought of almost getting caught made them a horny mess.

Instead of walking to my group of friends, who could still see us,

I sat down at her table with her friends, who didn't look up from their intense conversation about some Halloween party last night. Iza furrowed her eyebrows and sucked in a sharp breath as I pulled her into my lap.

"Wh-what are you doing?" she whisper-yelled.

Her friends paused and glanced over in our direction. "Did you hear that?"

I tightened my grip on her waist and ground my hips up against hers, my hard cock rubbing against her ass and making her a sopping wet mess. "They can't see you, Hellcat," I murmured into her ear.

"Wh—"

Before she could finish her sentence, I placed a hand over her mouth, drew her closer to me, and shushed her. "Don't say a word, unless … you want them to watch me fuck your pretty little pussy in public."

What were the chances that I'd see her last night and this morning? Slim to none.

I wasn't going to pass this opportunity up. I hadn't been able to stop thinking about her since last night. I almost hadn't wanted to leave. Her pussy felt so, so good. And those moans … damn, those moans had done something to me.

And if I believed in fate, I'd almost believe that was what this was.

Fate wasn't real, but lust was.

CHAPTER
SIX

IZA

I WIDENED my eyes even more and glanced over at my friends, who seemed to look right through me.

Jada shrugged her shoulders and snickered. "Probably just Iza getting railed by that sexy guy who followed her outside."

My entire body tensed, and I clenched. *Does ... does she know?*

After looping his feet around my ankles, Acaros spread my legs. My skirt rode up my thighs, and he dipped a hand between my legs, my underwear still soaked with his cum from last night. He ground his hips against mine, his bulge so big that it pressed against my entrance.

"Acaros," I whispered. "You shouldn't ..."

"Is this my cum?" he murmured, rubbing my wetness into my clit. "Still dripping out of your tight little hole? Didn't even think about showering after how much of a dirty"—he moved his fingers faster—"little"—he stopped moving his fingers and flicked one against my clit, sending me over the edge—"slut you were for me last night?"

I bit back a moan, my legs shaking so hard, the pleasure unbearable. Wave after wave after wave crashed through me.

He pressed his free hand against my mouth, his lips against my ear. "It's okay, Hellcat, you can moan for me, like I know you're desperate to do."

Another wall of pleasure hit me hard as he continued rubbing my pussy, and I moaned out into his hand, my eyes rolling back into my head. I clutched his hand, but my body seemed to move on its own against him.

Underneath me, as my pleasure slowly started to settle, his cock seemed like it was growing bigger and bigger. I glanced down to see that his bulge had grown, almost to the size of what I remembered his dick being last night in my fever dream.

"Let's pull out these tits," he said.

After tugging down my top, he pulled my tits right out of my bra and wrapped his large hands around them, his claws—*yes, claws* —digging into them. He fondled them, squeezing gently at first, but the closer he came to entering me, the more vicious he became.

Kneading. Groping. Squeezing them.

Hard.

Yet still, nobody looked over at me ... except a couple of glances from Acaros's friends.

Which, God, was so hot.

"Fuck, your tits are heavy," he murmured on my neck.

I arched my back against him, grinding my pussy against the head of his cock, and looked over at my friends, hoping they weren't seeing any of this. But the thought of them *almost* seeing something, of us *almost* being caught ...

Damn it ...

"Lean back against me," he ordered, pulling himself out of his pants.

With the lust finally seizing control of my last thread of sanity, I leaned back against him and rested my head on his muscular shoulder. The quiet hum of conversations inside the coffee shop drifted through my ears. He wrapped his strong arms underneath my thighs to pull them to my chest and then grabbed my tits again.

"Rub that pretty pussy for me while I fuck you in front of your friends."

I inhaled sharply, desperately trying to keep quiet, and hovered my fingers over my clit. He pressed the head of his cock against my entrance and shoved the first inch of his huge dick into my pussy. I stared down at it, eyes widening.

If this was real … there was no way that he'd fit inside me last night.

No way.

It wasn't even possible.

An inch and a half inside me, he released one of my legs, brought his hand up to his mouth, and licked it. Then, he rubbed it against my cunt, his saliva suddenly making my pussy drool with wetness.

"H-how did you—"

"Shh, shh, shh, Hellcat," he murmured, replacing his arm under my leg. He pushed another inch into me, this time with ease. "All you have to know is that I'm the only one who can turn your pussy into a puddle."

I curled my toes and clenched around him, my pussy hungry to swallow more of him.

He captured my nipples between his fingers and squeezed them, then slammed the rest of his huge cock into my pussy. My body jerked against him at the pressure inside me, but I smacked my lips together in hopes not to scream in pleasure.

"You're only mine," he said against my neck. "Mine."

He pounded up into me, my tits bouncing in his hands.

"Mine. Mine. Mine. Mine. Mine." His words left his mouth in quiet grunts every time he slammed into me, his stubble rubbing against my bare neck and tickling me. He groped my tits harder. "All mine." He moved a hand down to my pussy, placed it over mine, and forced me to slap my clit over and over. "Mine."

My eyes rolled back in my head, and I bit my lip hard to stop myself from moaning.

From screaming.

God, this felt way too good to be real. Way too fucking good.

I came once. Then twice a moment later. And then a third time in a row. Tremors rattled my body. I clutched his arm, desperate to hold on to something to steady myself. Yet he continued to pound into me, to bring me close and then over the edge again and again.

Until he finally slammed up into me one last time and came.

After his cock softened and slipped out of my pussy, cum drooling onto the floor, he stuffed four fingers into my cunt and then pulled them back out. Then, he shoved his cum-covered fingers into my mouth.

In a haze, I sucked on them hungrily.

"Taste familiar?" he murmured.

I swallowed the little he gave me of his cum and closed my eyes, the sweet taste of Fervor Crisp cream on my tongue. My eyes widened slightly, and I stiffened on his lap, looking back at him. Only for him not to be there anymore.

Wh-where did he go?

My gaze fell down my body, and I was dressed normally with my breasts back inside my shirt and my skirt pulled down. Wetness pooled between my thighs, and I gently pulled them apart, noticing the stickiness.

"Iza," Mikayla said, staring at me through wide eyes. "When did you get back?"

"What?" I said, voice muffled.

Jada giggled. "And why do you have a Fervor Crisp stuffed into your mouth like that?"

I reached up to pull a half-bitten Fervor Crisp from my mouth, finished chewing, and looked around the café for any sign of Acaros and his friends. But the seats across from us were now occupied by an elderly couple.

Acaros was nowhere to be found, but his dark chuckle drifted through the air.

"We'll meet again."

CHAPTER
SEVEN

ACAROS

A DARK PINK blanketed the night sky in the Kingdom of Lust. We had returned from Earth about seven hours ago, but it had already been too long. I inhaled the scent of roses that lined the walkways of the kingdom and leaned back in my seat.

Succubi and incubi danced around poles inside Rebel, a popular bar in Lust.

But none of them could hold my attention tonight.

I sipped on my Passion Delight and ran a hand over my face, wishing that I hadn't accepted Varoth's invitation to come out, but we were dining with the queen of Lust, her husband, Eros, and a couple of her playthings.

And nobody could say no to the queen.

The scent of cinnamon, mixed with apples, drifted in through the air, and then Eros appeared in the doorway that led to the patio area outside. I stared blankly ahead, watching Dani and Lucifer, the king of Pride, follow behind him, chatting quietly.

Dani, Eros, Lucifer, and a couple of high-standing demons in their court sat at the table.

"Acaros." Bazzon whistled.

Blankly, I glanced over at him. "What?"

"Eros asked you a question."

I shook my head, trying to get the thought of Iza out of it, then looked up at Eros. "Hmm?"

"Pussy that good?" Varoth said, squeezing my shoulders from behind, then taking a seat beside me. After a low chuckle, he looked over at Eros and smirked. "He's been high off lust since this morning."

I narrowed my eyes at Varoth, wishing that he'd drop it.

But if I had actually wanted him to drop it, if I had not really been into Iza, then when I had seen her this morning, I wouldn't have followed her out into the alleyway. And I really wouldn't have brought her back into the café to fuck her.

Though after last night and this morning, I couldn't get her out of my head.

Her sweet scent. Those eyes. How her breath quickened around me.

Incubi always had an effect on women, and I had made so many women's heart race, breath hitch. But I had felt nothing for them. Absolutely nothing until Iza. Until last night. Until her.

Eros curled his lips into a smirk. "Still getting off on your summoning?"

Dani leaned forward, breasts pressing against the table. "Do you have a crush?"

"No," I said sharply.

Because I didn't trust *any* demons. Sometimes not even my friends.

It didn't matter what kingdom a demon was from; they were all known to backstab each other for a plethora of reasons. If anyone saw Iza, they would do anything to have her in bed. Varoth and Bazzon had already commented on her this morning on the return through the portal.

My claws cut into my palms. I wanted to slice their throats open for it.

"It's not a crush. Just some good pussy." I sipped my Passion Delight. "Virgin."

"First time with a virgin?" Dani giggled. "Must've been good. You're blushing."

I dropped my mouth into a frown, but held back a growl so I didn't offend her. With half-angel, half-demon blood running through her veins, Dani was one of the most powerful beings in all of Hell. Her power comparable to God herself. Rumor had it that Dani was preparing to go to war with God after she captured one of God's angels last month.

"It was okay," I lied.

"Acaros met her again this morning," Varoth hummed. "She's so fucking hot."

Before I could even stop myself, I snapped my hand around his neck and squeezed. He had been one of my best friends since we had been mere children, but I had told him to drop her as the topic of our conversation in the portal.

Now this?

Dani giggled again, and I blew out a low breath and released my grip on him. After muttering an apology to the queen, I returned to my Passion Delight and glared at the roses just outside the patio.

I shouldn't fucking feel this way. She was a human—that was all.

"Why don't you relax with Qina?" Bazzon suggested, gesturing for Qina.

Not Qina. Anyone but Qina.

Qina danced at Rebel and for Dani at many of her gatherings and balls, and she'd had a major crush on me for years now.

"Acaros," Qina whispered, her voice like a snake traveling across the table as she approached us, her hips swaying side to side and a smirk painted across her red lips. "Seems I've been summoned to help you out a bit."

"I'm not interested tonight, Qina," I murmured.

"Oh, come on," Varoth taunted. "You're not falling for a human, are you?"

Nostrils flaring because I wasn't falling for any human, especially not one that I had only met last night and had zero connection with, I pushed my chair back. The legs scratched the stone floor underneath it. Then, I grabbed Qina's hand.

"We'll be in a Lust Room," I growled.

Qina giggled and followed after me, bouncing on her toes like the happiest fucking woman in the world because I, Acaros, was bringing her into a Lust Room—a place in demon bars where Lust demons could fuck—after years of sucking up to me and flirting nonstop with me, even after I showed her no interest.

But I didn't want Varoth and Bazzon pulling my fucking leg about a human anymore.

If I had to fuck Qina to prove it to them, then I would.

When we reached the Lust Rooms in the back of Rebel, I pushed one of the doors open and shoved her into the room. I locked it behind us and turned around to see Qina already pulling off her dress and climbing onto the bed.

I stared at her for a few moments, lip curling in disgust.

I didn't want to do this. I didn't want to be here.

"Acaros," she cooed, spreading her legs and showing me her pussy. "I know you like playing hard to get. Come here and take what you've wanted since we were kids. I can't wait to finally—"

"I don't know why they keep you around," I growled.

Her eyes widened, and she stood to walk closer to me. "Don't be like—"

Wrapping my hand around her throat, I lifted her into the air and glared at her, my eyes burning with anger. I didn't have any ounce of wrath inside me, as far as I was aware, but I couldn't stand this bitch. "If you lay a hand on me ever again, I'll lock you in the deepest pit in Hell. And my friends in Wrath won't think twice about tearing you to shreds."

"B-but—"

"And if you tell anyone that we *didn't* fuck in here tonight, I'll be sure to do it myself."

Qina's eyes widened. "Acaros ..."

After tossing her back down onto the bed, I opened a portal to

Earth and stepped through it. Fuck being in a Lust Room tonight with a girl I couldn't care less about, who would show no interest the moment I finished inside her.

I wanted Iza.

And tonight, I'd get her.

Again. And again. And again.

CHAPTER
EIGHT

IZA

GAZE LOCKED on to Jim Buffer, who stood in the middle of our living room, with his cock rock hard and swinging in a circle like a damn helicopter, I froze. What the hell was he doing here? Who the fuck had let him in? And why was he naked?!

"Mikayla!" I shouted through the apartment.

With bouncing orange hair, Mikayla walked into the living room, holding a tub of buttery popcorn. "Hey, Iza. What are you doing home so early? I thought you and Jada were staying out to study a bit more."

"I thought you were coming home to shower!" I exclaimed. "What are you doing?"

Even though Mikayla and I were having a full-blown conversation, Jim didn't even stop his dick swinging from side to side. A cross bounced on his chest, and he wore a dark pair of sunglasses that shielded his eyes.

"What the fuck?" I whispered under my breath. "It's like he doesn't even—"

"See you?" Mikayla said. "He doesn't. Can't hear us either."

While Mikayla stared at the naked man who had bullied her for years with a smug smirk on her face, I stared at *her* like she was crazy because ... *what the fuck?!* Why was there a naked man in the middle of our living room who couldn't see or hear us?

"Why?!" I exclaimed when she didn't expand.

"Oh, um ..." Mikayla rocked back on her heels. "Just a condition he has."

"Since when?"

She shrugged. "Don't know. I found him in the hallway."

"So you brought him into our house?!" I asked, fucking flabbergasted as he jumped up onto the couch next to Mikayla and began thrusting wildly toward her face, his dick flopping and smacking against his abdomen and then thigh. "Why?!"

"Holy shit." Jada walked into the room and leaned closer to me. "Do you see this too?"

"Yes, I see it."

"Why is Jim Buffer naked in our living room and pelvic-thrusting worse than your ex?"

Mikayla rolled her eyes. "For the last time, I found him in the hallway."

Jada arched a brow and crossed her arms. "You just randomly found a naked guy wearing a pair of sunglasses, pelvic-thrusting in the hallway of a building that only has three apartments and *his* isn't one of them?"

"Actually, he was doing the helicopter when I walked in," I hummed, biting back a giggle.

After clearing her throat, Mikayla nodded. "Yep."

"What kind of voodoo shit did you do to him?" Jada asked.

"Come on, Jay," Mikayla said, tugging on one of her coiled strands of orange hair. It bounced next to her face and got caught in her black-framed glasses. "You know I can't do any voodoo or magic. That was apparent after last night."

Yeah ... about that.

Instead of anyone responding, we all stayed quiet, the tension building between us.

After looking over at me, Jada drew her tongue over her teeth. It was as if we were all waiting for the other person to say something. At least, I knew that I was because how the hell could I explain that a demon—a freaking sex demon!—had shown up in my room last night and stolen my virginity? And then fucked me again today in public, but somehow, my body was invisible so nobody could see it?!

The first part was at least somewhat plausible, but the part about invisibility was …

Way out there.

"Are we not going to talk about the elephant in the room?" Jada asked.

"You mean the naked guy?" I asked.

Jim rocked his hips aggressively back and forth, his arms up and his fingers tucked behind his ears. Those sunglasses were slowly sliding down his face with every thrust, until they fell off into Mikayla's lap. Eyes filmed over, he stared emptily at the wall.

"No, not him," Jada said. "The fact that we actually did summon some shit last night."

Mikayla burst out in laughter for a moment, and then she looked at our faces and pressed her lips together. I chewed on my inner cheek, heart pounding at the thought of that man—*that demon*—who had snuck into my bed.

"That didn't happen," Mikayla said. "Right, Iza?"

"I, um …" I whispered. "I had someone visit me last night and take my virginity."

"Whoa," Jim said, nodding along. "Nice. Not a virgin anymore. Does that mean—"

"Your dick is small," Jada snarled at him. "Get out of our house."

Jim had awoken from his naked, thrusting slumber, if you could even call it that, and glanced over at Jada, then at me, then down at his own body. His eyes widened, and he grabbed one of our nice pillows to cover his dick.

I frowned because I always fell asleep with that pillow on the couch, but decided that my face would never even want to touch that thing now that it was pressed against Jim's grimy dick and hairy balls.

"Wh-what's going on?" he cried. "Where are my clothes?!"

Jada grabbed him by the ear and tugged him toward the door. "Don't know. Don't care."

"What am I doing here? How am I going to get home?" Jim cried.

She threw him out into the hall. "Again, don't know and don't care."

"Wait!" Mikayla shouted, tossing his sunglasses to Jada. "Don't forget this!"

Once Jada threw his glasses at his feet, she slammed the door in Jim's face and twirled around on her heel.

"Mikayla," Jada said, blowing out a breath through her nose. "I don't know what kind of weird sunglasses-wearing, ugly, naked man kink you have going on, but you need to explain what the hell went on last night because that was my favorite pillow, and now, it has his dick juices all over it."

"It was mine too," I hummed.

Mikayla rocked back on her heels. "I don't know what's going on."

Jada raised both her eyebrows. "Is that why you had a bowl of popcorn, about to watch the guy who had bullied you for three years embarrass himself instead of sending him on his way back to his home?"

Chewing on her lip, Mikayla rocked back. "Maybe ..."

"Start talking," Jada said.

I leaned closer to her, desperate to know that I wasn't the only one being haunted or possessed or whatever the hell they called it. How had those demons found us last night? Had it really been by the Ouija board?

"Okay," Mikayla whispered. "Okay. Okay. I'll tell you everything."

Thunder suddenly crashed overhead, and the sky turned dark through the windows. For the second night in a row, the power turned out, and suddenly, Mikayla and Jada were frozen in time. Mikayla's mouth was open, as if she was in the middle of a sentence, and Jada's brows were scrunched.

And then I saw those piercing red eyes in the middle of the darkness, staring at me from my bedroom door.

CHAPTER
NINE

ACAROS

BREED.

As soon as my gaze landed on Iza, standing in the middle of her living room with her friends, who I had frozen in time, the thought raced through my mind over and over again. I stalked closer to her, my dick throbbing.

"Wh-what are you doing here?" she whispered, shaking her head. "How'd you—"

"Bend over the couch and arch your back."

She stared at me in bewilderment. "What?!"

"Bend over the couch and arch your back," I ordered. "Now."

Pressing her legs together, Iza glanced toward her frozen friends and then back toward me. "Right here? B-but my friends ... and I ... we just saw each other ..." She fumbled more and more on her words, the closer I approached.

Heavens, I'm going to fucking breed her until her belly is swollen.

My dick hardened even more, my balls heavy and warm against my thigh. A guttural growl escaped my throat, and I closed the distance between us, seizing her lips, spinning her around, and bending her over the couch myself.

An indescribable need to take Iza rocked through me, one that I had never experienced before. Not with another demon and definitely not with a human. I grasped her hips tighter and pulled her closer to me.

Wanting to get as deep as possible, as soon as possible.

And not wanting to pull out at all.

Iza made no move to push me away, to curse me out, or to simply say *no*. So, I curled my talons around her panties and ripped them straight off her body. She inhaled sharply and stared back at me, her pussy drooling.

"I ... I haven't been able to stop thinking about you all day," she whispered.

I slammed deep into her pussy and grunted.

She couldn't say shit like that to me and expect me to hold back on her. I hadn't gotten the thought of her out of my fucking head since last night. The craving was growing bigger, the desire to be inside her whenever I had the chance ...

I pounded into her pussy, talons digging into her ass cheeks and tongue gliding against my sharp teeth. My horns ached, but the need to dump a load of my cum inside her surpassed the desire for her to stroke the long, rigid horns on my head.

"Fuck," I hissed, the urge becoming unbearable.

If I fucked her any harder, I would hurt her. After all, she was a weak human who I should want nothing to do with. But I continued to slam into her repeatedly, her pussy tightening around my throbbing cock.

I dropped my head and squeezed my eyes shut, needing to push the thought out of my head and to slow down so I wouldn't hurt her. Yet the harder I closed my eyes, the more pressure rose up inside me.

"Breed," I murmured underneath my breath. "Breed now."

Iza tightened on me. "Wh-what?"

"I need to breed you," I growled, pounding myself into her harder. My hands tightened around her waist, and I didn't pull more than two inches out of her at any point from there on out because my cum was supposed to be buried inside her pussy. "I need to breed you now."

After sucking in a breath, Iza glanced back at me, and her pussy began gushing around me like a fucking waterfall. Her cunt even wetter than any other succubus that I had been with.

"Y-you c-can't b-breed me," she cried.

But she arched her back and continued to tighten her pussy around me.

"I need to," I grunted. "I can't fucking stop now."

She grabbed at the pillows on the couch, fingers dipping into them and moans escaping past her lips. "Y-you can't! I ... this ..." She looked around the room, brows drawn together in pleasure. "This isn't real. You're not—"

Before she could finish her sentence, I pushed her head against the couch cushion to arch her back harder and so I could get deeper inside her and thrust even faster inside that tight, sopping cunt.

With one side of her head pressed against the cushion, she stared back at me. Her tits swung against the couch, hitting it every time I slammed into her, swaying back and forth and back and forth and—

Fuuuuck ...

"Beg for me to breed you," I demanded.

I always focused on my partner's pleasure before mine, especially a human's ... yet right now, I could barely even focus at all. The desire—*the need*—had built up quickly inside me, and all I could focus on was breeding her. Filling up her pussy. Making more of me, more of us.

"You ..." she started, mouth forming an O. "You have to ... to s-s-t—"

I stilled deep in her pussy, wrapped my arms underneath her legs, then fastened my hands around the back of her neck, putting her in a full nelson position. Under my complete control.

She could beg me not to breed her, not to cum inside her, but she had no control anymore. She didn't have a say. There was no stopping me.

"Don't stop!" she cried, helpless in my arms.

Her legs began trembling hard, and I turned so she faced her friends, who were completely oblivious to the fact that their room-mate was being pounded by a seven-foot demon who was hungry to get her pregnant.

"Come inside me!" she cried, staring over at her friends, who were stopped in time. "B-breed m-me."

Over and over and over, I pounded up into her tight pussy. My dick was throbbing inside of her, my balls heavy and warm, filled with cum that I refused to dump anywhere besides inside her aching little cunt.

I'd make sure that not even a drip dribbled out of that hole.

Because her holes had been fucking made to be filled.

Because her holes were begging for cum.

Because her holes made her my needy, cum-hungry, breedable bitch.

Another moan left her mouth, and suddenly, my cum was spilling out into her pussy.

"Fuck!" she screamed, pussy swallowing every drop of my cum. "Give me more! More!"

While I just dumped all I had inside her, I continued to pound up into that pussy over and over and over, my dick hardening almost immediately from her cunt and my balls becoming heavier by the second.

"Take that fucking dick like a good girl," I murmured. "Show me how much you want it."

Panting, she attempted to buck her hips against mine, back and forth and around my throbbing cock. I wanted to hold out, to fuck her harder for a few more minutes, but her tits were bouncing against my forearms and her pussy clamped down on my dick so tightly that if I pulled it out one more time, I feared she might rip it off.

I slammed myself into her and stilled, breathing unsteadily against her shoulder and waiting for her grip on my dick to loosen. But another moan left her mouth, and she exploded around me, pussy pulsing around my cum-covered dick.

"Fuck," I grunted, letting her body fall forward slightly so she was at a ninety-degree angle with my body. I slammed deeper into her, past her cervix, and filled up her pussy with another thick load of my cum. "I'm going to breed you like this every fucking day, Iza."

CHAPTER
TEN

IZA

WITH MY PUSSY filled up with cum, I fell forward onto the couch and breathed heavily. I didn't know what had come over me a second ago, but I had been begging for all of Acaros's cum. Every last damn drop of it.

And when I opened my eyes, that man wouldn't even be here.

Because I had been dreaming this all up. Because he wasn't real. Because how could someone freeze time, make us invisible, and turn into a demon? It was against all laws of science and reality ever!

"I need to wake up," I murmured when I finally came down from my high. "Wake up."

I dragged a hand across my face and finally blinked my eyes open, half expecting to be in my bedroom and half expecting to be half naked in front of Mikayla and Jada, humping the pillow, like Jim had been a half hour ago.

But when my eyes adjusted to the light—*or lack thereof*—I squinted and stared into the devilish eyes of Acaros. He stood in front of the living room window, the moonlight shining around his huge and muscular body and gleaming off his horns.

Hell, why am I still in this stupid dream?

There was absolutely zero chance that a man who looked as good as he did would ever want to be with me. No man as tall, as muscular, and as handsome had ever even looked in my direction twice, which definitely meant that I was dreaming.

"Wake up, Iza," I repeated, sitting up and staring into those glowing red eyes. "Wake up."

"Why do you keep repeating that?"

"Because you're not real."

"What did you just say?" he growled, suddenly … angry?

My God, I really am going crazy. Now, I'm thinking this delusion is mad at me.

"I said, you're not real." I hopped off the couch and pulled on some clothes so Mikayla and Jada wouldn't find me naked when I finally woke back up. "How can you be? You show up at the most random times, freeze time itself, and make me invisible to my friends."

He stepped toward me, his cock hanging between his legs,—so freaking enormous that it nearly came to his knees. I forced myself to look back up at his face. Another reason why I was dreaming. If he had actually put that inside me, I'd be dead.

So, I slapped myself across the face. "Wake the hell up, Iza."

"Don't do that," he growled, now at my side and pulling my hand away from my cheek.

"You know what it is?" I murmured to myself. "Someone must've drugged me."

"Nobody drugged you." His voice dropped. "And if they did, I would kill them."

"Well then, maybe I should check myself into the psych ward because I know that there isn't a seven-foot-tall, muscular-as-hell demon standing in my living room with two loads of his cum dripping down my thighs right—"

Wait …

I glanced down to see thick strands of Acaros's cum coating my inner thighs. A snarl escaped his throat, and then his fingers were scooping up the cum on my legs and thrusting it back up into me. I shrieked and gripped on to his shoulder.

"If I'm going to breed you, then you're going to keep my cum inside your cunt."

My eyes widened, and I sucked in another sharp breath. *What the hell is happening?!*

"You're not real," I repeated. "This is a dream."

"What is it going to take for you to believe me, Iza? Do I have to get you pregnant?"

Somehow, my eyes widened even more. Warmth exploded between my thighs as he continued to push more and more of his cum back up into my cunt, as if he really did want to get me pregnant. Me, an average-to-ugly-looking human who had been a virgin last night!

"Your pussy is tightening around my fingers," he noted. "Seems so."

After shoving his hand away from me, I pressed my thighs together and crossed my arms over my chest. My cheeks burned in embarrassment, yet I couldn't show him that. This man might've been in my dream, but the humiliation was real.

"I do not need you to get me pregnant."

His red eyes seemed to glow even brighter. "Does the thought of it fulfill something in you?"

The warmth grew even hotter inside me, my nipples hardening against my forearm.

Did the thought of him getting me pregnant fulfill something inside me? Of course it didn't! I definitely didn't feel wanted and desired for the first time in my life. Psh, the thought of someone liking me so much that they got me pregnant was deranged and not attractive at all …

"It fulfills something inside me," he growled, seizing my chin and forcing me to look up at him. "Something I can't explain, but it's sinister, Iza." He drew the pad of his thumb across my lower lip. "I *need* to breed you."

"No," I whispered, "you don't."

Yes, the hell he does.

"You let me inside," he murmured. "You've wanted this from the beginning too."

"You let yourself inside my room last night!" I exclaimed. "Not the other way around."

"The only way an incubus can claim his prey is if the prey desires it," he said.

But what the hell even was an incubus?! Was that some kind of demon that he was?

He popped his thumb right into my mouth. "There's no hiding your excitement from me, no matter how hard you press those legs together, Iza. I can smell you from miles away." He dipped his head, his nose against my ear. "How'd you think I found you this morning?"

After shaking my head, I pushed him away for good. "You're a dream."

The smirk that had blessed his lips suddenly disappeared.

He clenched his jaw hard. "If this is how you want to play, Iza, then fine."

A moment later, the lights suddenly flickered back on, and Acaros was gone from the living room. I stared at the slightly open window with wide eyes, both wishing that he hadn't left and that I hadn't pushed him away in my dream.

"You good?" Jada asked, arching her brow at me.

Mikayla snickered. "Why are you standing like that? It looks like you have to pee."

I glanced down at my body to see my legs pressed together, the same way I had been standing, trying to hold in all of Acaros's cum. I swallowed hard and loosened my stiffened stance, only to feel the rush of thick, gooey wetness between my thighs.

Hell ... what if that wasn't a dream? What if Acaros is real?

CHAPTER
ELEVEN

IZA

"I'M GOING TO GET PREGNANT," I whispered.

Because someway, somehow, I knew that the wetness between my thighs wasn't pee from pissing myself because that demon had scared the shit out of me. No ... no, it was his thick cum dripping down my inner thighs.

Jada laughed. "Calm your tits, Iza. You're still a virgin."

Mikayla widened her eyes. "Right?"

I scooped the cum off my thighs and stared at it for a few moments because I couldn't wrap my head around the fact that this wasn't just my pee. Thick, gooey, and white. It had to be cum, dripping out from my pussy.

After cupping my vagina, I hurried to the bathroom and slammed the door. More and more cum poured out of my hole, and no matter how hard I tried to clench to keep it inside—not that I wanted it to stay inside—it wouldn't stop.

"Oh my God!" I exclaimed.

"Are you okay?" Jada asked, banging on the door.

"No!"

"What's wrong?" Mikayla said.

"What's wrong is that there is cum pouring out of my pussy and it won't stop!"

They mumbled behind the door, then suddenly, the door flew open from Jada's kick and slammed against the sink counter. I hovered over the toilet with my pants bunched around my ankles and my hand still cupping my pussy.

Cum leaked between my fingers and into the toilet. I shrieked and replaced my cum-covered hand with my clean one in hopes to stop it. Not sure how that was supposed to happen, but it needed to as soon as possible!

"Oh my God," Jada said. "There's so much."

"Daaaamn!" Mikayla murmured. "These demons are good."

Jada cut her gaze to Mikayla, then snatched Mikayla's ear with her two sharply manicured Halloween-themed fingers. "What the hell is going on?! Why does Iza have cum pouring out of her vagina?"

"I can explain. I can explain," Mikayla said, wincing. "Just release me."

With her nostrils flared, Jada shoved Mikayla away from me and crossed her arms.

"Last night ..." Mikayla chewed on her bottom lip. "I think we summoned sex demons."

"Fuck," I whispered, the cum slowly stopping from leaking out of me.

If we had really summoned sex demons, then ... then Acaros was real. And if Acaros was real, then this was his cum leaking out of my pussy. And if this was his cum leaking out of my pussy, then he might really have a shot at getting me pregnant.

Jada turned toward me. "Is that why you have about three gallons of cum inside you?"

I looked between her and Mikayla, then nodded. "H-he ... I ..."

While my mouth was open, I didn't even know how to begin. It was crazy enough that demons were ninety-nine percent real, but to tell them that he could make us invisible and stop time and all this other crazy shit, like having three gallons of cum stored up inside him?!

"H-he j-just came to ..." I whispered.

"Oh Lord." Jada grabbed a towel and began wiping the cum off my thighs. "He broke her."

"I didn't believe him, so he said he'd get me pregnant to show me that he was real."

"Daaaamn!" Mikayla said, excited.

Jada hurled the cum-covered towel at her. "Go brew her a cup of tea, you crazy witch."

Mikayla dumped the towel into the hamper and scurried out of the bathroom. "I didn't mean it!" she called from down the hall. "You know, I would apologize, but I'm too jealous that he has visited you multiple times!"

After glancing up at me, Jada furrowed her brows. "Has he?"

I swallowed hard and nodded. "Three."

"Fuck."

"Yeah, and he's done that three times now too."

"Shit," Jada cursed. "The one that visited me only came once."

My eyes widened slightly because for the first time since last night, I didn't feel crazy.

"When did it happen?" she asked.

"Last night. This morning at the café. And just now."

"How'd it happen just now?" Jada asked. "You were right in front of us the whole time."

"He can ... he can stop time," I whispered. "And make people invisible."

"Probably has some other powers too," Mikayla said, already back with the tea.

"How the hell did you get back so quickly?" Jada asked.

Mikayla rocked back on her heels, curly red hair bouncing around her shoulders.

Once Jada rolled her eyes and muttered, "You have some explaining to do," she retrieved a clean pair of pants from my bedroom.

I walked to the living room and collapsed onto the couch, not caring anymore that Jim had just been humping it with his crusty dick.

"I'm going to get pregnant."

"You're not going to get pregnant," Jada said. "Aren't demons, like, dead or something?"

"Those are vampires," I said.

"Yeah, but same thing, right, Mikayla?"

"Statistically speaking," Mikayla started.

Jada held up her hand. "Some bullshit 'bout to come out of your mouth, huh?"

"No," Mikayla said. "I'm just saying that statistically speaking with all that cum inside her, she may very likely get pregnant because sex demons not only have a lot of sperm, but their sperm is very strong."

"Some bullshit," Jada murmured. "Told you."

"He told me he is going to breed me," I whispered. "And I liked it."

"Daaaamn."

Jada hurled a pillow at Mikayla so hard that it sent her flying across the room and slamming into the wall. When she fell to the ground, there was a huge Mikayla-sized indent in the wall. My eyes widened.

"Wh-what was that?" I asked.

Jada stared down at her hands in shock. "I ... don't know."

Mikayla hopped up like that blast hadn't just affected her and dusted herself off. "I do." She grabbed her purse from the stand near the door. "But I think it would be better if I brought you somewhere to explain. Our apartment is now cursed with sex demons, who will come and go as they please, and we can't have another Iza situation on our hands. Follow me."

"I'm not stepping out of this damn house unless I know where we're going," Jada said.

"We're going to a nightclub," Mikayla said, already out the door, "called The Lounge."

CHAPTER
TWELVE

IZA

"ARE you sure we're going to the right place?" I asked.

Tucked away in an alley behind Crimson's Bakery, this Lounge place had one gray metal door that apparently led into a nightclub and not a serial killer's basement. Jada crossed her arms and arched a brow while Mikayla banged on the door twice.

After a moment, an enormously muscular man opened the door. He stared down at Mikayla and then stepped out of the way, nodding as if he recognized her. We walked down a deserted hallway, then down a set of dusty stairs, a single light flickering above us.

The low thump of music played through the walls, and I grabbed Jada's hand because I didn't trust Mikayla.

Don't ask why my dumbass continues to follow her to my death.

First, she had known about demons; next, she was bringing us to a discreet, creepy club.

When we reached the bottom of the stairs, Mikayla opened another door. Inside, there was a bar in the center of the room, filled with people flirting with each other. Twelve beige-cushioned booths sat around the perimeter of the room. Everything was lit with dim red lights, which hung off of the brick walls.

All the women were dressed in skimpy little dresses or short skirts, and my legging-wearing ass felt way too out of place. But I hadn't wanted to change into a skirt before we left because I feared that I'd have another explosion of cum in my pussy again.

"What the hell is this place?" Jada asked, following Mikayla to an empty booth.

"The Lounge."

After we sat in a booth, Jada reached across the table and grabbed Mikayla by the collar. "You'd better start talking now. We got all the way here and still haven't even had a sentence of an explanation."

"Okay, so let me start by saying that this is a demon bar."

"What?!" I exclaimed, causing people to look over at us.

"Shh," she said. "All I said is that this is a demon bar."

"Why are we here then?" Jada asked. "And how'd we get in?"

"Well, after I cast that spell last night ..." she started, chewing on the inside of her cheek. "I might've caught the attention of a sorcerer of dark magic. He showed up in my room last night after the sex demon and demanded to know where I learned the magic."

Jada stared at Mikayla blankly. "Stop playin'."

"If Iza can be haunted by a demon who makes her invisible and stuffs her with cum, then why don't you believe that I am—maybe —a powerful witch?" Mikayla asked, pushing some hair behind her shoulder. "Come on. I even look like one."

I rested my elbows on the table and drew my hands across my face. "Oh my God."

"So, how'd we get in here?" Jada asked.

"Demons fear me." Mikayla shrugged. "I'm kind of a big deal now."

I slid out of the booth. "I need a drink."

Once I fast-walked to the bar because I really didn't want to go up here alone, I stopped near the only other human-looking person in The Lounge with chocolate-brown hair that cascaded down her shoulders and pretty hazel eyes.

Mikayla was crazy.

Truly insane.

"What's your name?" the woman suddenly asked.

If I didn't know any better and if I actually believed in the supernatural, then I would almost say that she didn't belong here. She seemed too innocent, almost angelic. But if what Mikayla said was true about this club, then she was a demon too.

"Iza," I said quietly, not wanting a whole conversation with another demon.

Last time that had happened, three gallons of cum had been buried in my pussy.

"I'm Dani." She held out her hand. "Nice to meet you."

After swallowing some anxiety, I gently shook her hand.

"What're you doing here?" she asked.

"My friend dragged me here," I said, glancing over my shoulder. "You?"

She paused for a moment, then glanced down the bar at two men—one with piercing green eyes and a devilishly handsome face and the other with white hair that came to his shoulders and eyes an icy blue. "Having fun."

"Well," I hummed, sensing the same lusty feelings I had felt earlier within her. And props to her for scoring both of those handsome guys, but I needed to run right out of here and never go anywhere with Mikayla again. "I should, um, leave you then."

After following the bartender to the other side of the bar that was empty—thank God—I stood on my toes and leaned across the bar. "Excuse me." When he didn't turn around, I cleared my throat and spoke a bit louder. "Excuse me, can I get some water?"

He twisted around, his full lips pulled into a small smirk. "Just a water?"

"Yes, just a water."

"You don't want to try our signature Passion Delight?" he offered, dipping a clean straw into the drink he had just finished making and holding it to my lips. "Here, have a sip. It's sweet and one of our most popular drinks."

Last time I'd tried something that I wasn't necessarily super familiar with, it'd ended up being made with cum! Those damn Fervor Crisps.

But I just wanted to get back to the table before someone else approached me, so I wrapped my lips around it.

The sweetness immediately hit my taste buds. I closed my eyes and suddenly saw Acaros standing over me, the head of his dick against my lips and his sweet cum rolling down the back of my throat. Warmth gushed between my thighs.

I snapped my eyes open and took a huge breath. "Water, please."

"Ah, too bad," the bartender flirted. "I'll be right back."

When he headed down to Dani to give her the Passion Delight, I turned around and scanned the club for any sign of Acaros. In the back of The Lounge, a group of huge guys were turned in my direction. While I couldn't see their faces, I could feel their stares.

Fuck.

"Your water," the bartender said behind me.

I grabbed my water off the counter. "Thanks!"

Without speaking another word, I twirled around toward my table and slammed right into a hard chest. After cursing under my breath and hoping that it wasn't Acaros, I craned my head up to stare into blazing black eyes.

Don't ask me how black eyes could be blazing, but they were.

"You're new here," the guy hummed.

I giggled nervously and bit back the urge to say that I would never be returning. "Yeah."

He leaned against the counter. "Two Passion Delights—for me and the lovely little lady."

Waving my hand at him, I shook my head. "Oh, no. I'm good."

His thumb swiped across my lower lip. "It's just a drink, sweetheart."

"I have water." I glanced over his shoulder. "Besides, my friends are waiting for me."

When I circled around him, he snatched my wrist. "Just on—"

Before he could finish his sentence, someone snapped their hand around his throat, and the demon was suddenly hurled across the club. Another demon stood in front of me, the muscles in his back rippling.

"Daaaamn!" Mikayla shouted at our table.

My eyes widened, and I slowly lifted my gaze to meet the back of Acaros's head.

CHAPTER
THIRTEEN

ACAROS

"THIS OUGHT TO BE FUN," Dani, the queen of lust, hummed as I stormed past her.

After Amon crashed into the wall, he stood up and dusted himself off, a low growl escaping through his jagged teeth, his demon finally emerging. Envy—though an unfamiliar emotion—rushed through me.

He'd touched her.

He'd touched Iza.

My fist collided with Amon's jaw, and he crumpled to the ground. With my hand around his throat to keep him in place, I picked him up into the air and slammed another balled fist into his cheekbone.

"Acaros!" Iza cried behind me. "What are you doing?!"

Why had she come down to The Lounge tonight? Only demons and a few paranormal creatures knew about this place. She should've never been able to find it. But now, she was standing behind me, getting hit on by every fucking demon in here.

I slammed my fist into that fucker's face again, sending him flying into a table. The bartender came around the front of the bar, placing a hand on my chest and warning me not to cause any more trouble or else he'd banish me from coming back.

Iza suddenly appeared by my side. "What is wrong with you?!"

"I'm taking care of a fucking problem."

"How was he a problem to you?"

"He fucking touched you," I snarled, grabbing a Passion Delight off the counter. "That's how he's a problem to me, Iza." I took a swig of it, hoping that it'd calm me down. "What are you fucking doing here anyway?"

I had come here to blow off some steam after she pissed me off back at her place, to convince myself that this was some sort of—what humans called—crush, that I didn't care if she believed that I was real or not, and that I didn't *really* want to get her pregnant.

My dick stiffened inside my pants at the thought of getting this hellcat of a woman pregnant with my child—a demon—which would forge a bond between us forever. I gritted my teeth and cursed underneath my breath, getting harder.

"What are you doing here?" I repeated, a second away from losing it … and asking for a Lust Room, where I would pound that pretty body into a bed all night.

"I … you really are a demon," she whispered, gazing up at my head. "Your horns …"

Because if she stared at my horns for one more second with those huge brown eyes, I'd ask her to touch them. I grabbed her by the elbow and dragged her out of the center of the room and toward the back, where there was a bit more privacy.

"You shouldn't be here," I said.

"My friend brought me here," she said, glancing over her shoulder.

After following her gaze, I saw that cursed woman with curly, bright red hair, who had murmured that summons with the Ouija board on Halloween night, smirking at us. Iza's other friend sat to the redhead's right, looking at Varoth.

Iza must've noticed the lust oozing from her friend, too, because a sudden waft of pleasure drifted from Iza's pussy and through my nose. I grunted and closed my eyes, needing to leave before I lost complete control around her.

"Let's go," I said, guiding her to the exit.

"B-but my friends—"

"I'll return you safely to them tomorrow."

I continued to pull her toward the exit.

She pressed her heels into the ground. "Where are you taking me?"

"To my place."

To my place?!

Out of all the places I can take her, I decide to bring her home?! What will I do with her?

I didn't know.

I had never brought a woman back to my place before, not in Hell and definitely not here on Earth either. But if I didn't get her out of here quickly, then I was going to lose it with my buddies chuckling at how whipped I was for a human—which I wasn't—and with how many other demons flirting with her tonight.

"Why do you think I'd go anywhere with you?" she exclaimed.

After twirling around to face her, I pushed the door open and snatched her jaw in my hand. "Because if you don't leave with me right here, right now, then I'm going to fuck you in front of every demon here. Claim you as my own. And I won't use my magic to hide you this time. Everyone will see how much you're mine."

CHAPTER
FOURTEEN

IZA

PERCHED on the top floor of one of the tallest buildings in the city, Acaros's home was *nothing* like mine with floor-to-ceiling windows, an apartment more luxurious than anything I had seen, and a goddamn pool on his private rooftop.

"This is your home?" I asked, staring at the high-rise in awe.

"Here."

"What do you mean, here?"

"On Earth, this is my home."

"Where else would you …"

He released my hand. "I usually spend my nights in Hell, not on Earth."

My eyes widened slightly. *Oh.*

After scavenging through his refrigerator, he pulled out a black cardboard box and handed it to me, along with a beer bottle that had *Passion Delight* written across the label in pink letters. "Sit on the couch and eat."

I peered into the box to see those Fervor Crisps from yesterday—or was it this morning?! My days were getting so mixed up with this man—sitting in the container, white powder on the flaky dough.

"You want me to eat these?" I asked, sitting on the couch.

He sat beside me. "I assumed you were hungry. Your stomach was growlin—"

"These have cum in them!" I exclaimed.

"And?"

"And?" I repeated back, shaking my head. "Do you not find that weird?"

"No."

"No?! There is cum in them!"

"If you don't want to eat them, then I will." He scooped one up in his hand and took a huge bite of it, the creamy goodness dripping onto his full lips. He opened up the beer bottle and took a swig.

The sweet scent drifted through my nostrils, and I recognized it as that lust drink from The Lounge. He tilted the bottle toward me, and for some gosh-darn reason, I grabbed it from him and took a sip.

Pleasure flooded through my body as I swallowed down the liquid. And I found myself leaning closer to him, my breasts on his forearm. He stiffened and looked down at my tits pressed against his body.

"Iza," he growled. "Be careful with what you do around me."

"Can I see them?" I whispered.

"Can you see what?"

My heart pounded in my chest, and I lifted my gaze from his blazing eyes to his head, nervous to say the wrong thing and nervous that if I did say the wrong thing, he'd flip out on me the way that he had on that other demon tonight.

"You want to see my horns?" he concluded.

Cheeks burning, I turned my head to the window. "Maybe …"

Before we had left The Lounge, he had returned to his normal human-looking self.

He lifted the Passion Delight to my lips again. "Take another sip."

I sipped the drink again, my pussy warm and pulsing now.

After he inhaled deeply, his eyes began darkening even more, and those horns … God, those horns began growing from his forehead. Long, curled, black, and covered with ridges. More warmth spread through my body.

"Come up here," he said, pulling me into his lap.

In awe, I grazed my fingers up his horns, the almost leather-like material feeling so good on the pads of my fingers. I pressed my pussy against the bulge in his pants, whimpering softly, and took hold of them, making him grunt.

Yes, grunt.

The sexiest sound I had heard in my life.

"Fuck, Iza," he growled. "You're a natural."

Wanting to pleasure him even more, I stroked one of his huge horns, breathing heavily.

"Just like that, Hellcat. You're doing so, so good for me."

I held back another whimper and chewed on my inner cheek.

For heaven's sake, Acaros was a sex demon! And here I was, giving him pleasure.

He must've brought loads of women here to sleep with every night, probably told them all the same things that he had been telling me, filled them with gallons of cum, and promised to get them all pregnant too.

I peeked down at him, body suddenly burning with jealousy.

I couldn't have been the only woman that he'd ever said stuff like that to, and it pissed me off that I had fallen so much under his charm that I agreed to come back to his place tonight with him. How stupid was I?

My hand tightened around his horn, and he grunted lowly.

But all I could think about was how hundreds of women had probably asked to see his horns, drawn their fingers up each of them like they were the most magical things in the world, and then became so horny that they climbed up in his lap.

Jealousy pooled through my body. I snapped myself out of the trance he had put me in.

I jumped off him, grabbed my purse, and headed to the door. "I'm going home."

"What?" he asked, confusion washing over his face.

"I'm going home," I said, opening the door. "Don't follow—"

He slapped his large hand over the door and snapped it closed, his elongated claws digging into the wood. "You're not going anywhere. Not in this town. Not at this time of night. And not without me."

"Move your hand." I snapped my hands around his wrist and pulled as hard as I could in an attempt to get him to move. But he didn't budge even a millimeter. Not even a damn millimeter! "I'm going home, Acaros."

"Not tonight."

I twirled around to face him. "Well, I'll wait until you fall asleep, and then I'll sneak out."

"I'd like to see you try."

After glaring at him for another moment, I tore my gaze away and fixed it on the marble floor of this man's—*this demon's*—multi-million-dollar high-rise in the middle of the city. "How many other women have you brought home?"

His dark eyes widened, but then a smirk crossed his beautiful face. "Is that what this is?"

"What?"

"Envy."

"No!" *Yes.* "I just don't want to get WSDD."

"The fuck is WSDD?"

I crossed my arms. "Weird sex demon disease."

"First of all, *Hellcat*, sex demons don't carry any diseases trans-mittable to humans." He moved closer, his huge body looming over mine. "The only thing that we can do to a human is get her pregnant."

My entire body stiffened, and the warmth spread between my legs again. *Pregnant.*

Why did he just throw around that word like he *wanted* to actually do that to me? He had talked about how much he wanted to breed me the other night, and now ... he was mentioning pregnancy again.

"I bet you get tons of girls pregnant, don't you?" I asked to shut off this raging lust switch in my head that screamed at me to shove him back onto the couch, crawl up into his lap, and fuck him over and over and over again.

His lips curled into a devious smirk. "So, this is envy."

"No, it's not."

He stalked closer to me, and I stepped back, hitting the door.

"You want to know how many humans I've gotten pregnant?" he asked.

I glared up at him, nipples taut behind my crossed arms. *Hell no.* "Yes."

"Well, Iza," he hummed, one forearm on the door above my head and his opposite hand hovering over my pussy through my pants. He just barely glided his fingers over my slit. "If all goes to plan, you'll be the first and only."

CHAPTER
FIFTEEN

IZA

"Y-YOUR F-FIRST AND ONLY?" I squeaked, head craned up to look him in the eye.

Standing at seven feet, maybe even taller with those horns, he loomed over me. "Yes."

There was no hesitation in his voice. Not a freaking ounce.

"So, you're going to walk back over to the couch, crawl up onto my lap, and get yourself off like a good girl for me." He lifted my chin. "Do you understand me, Hellcat?"

I pressed my thighs together and sucked in a breath, pussy pounding. "Yes." The word came out in a breathy whisper because I feared if I said it any louder, I'd moan it.

Heat coursed through my body, entire body beating, throbbing, aching for him to touch me again. He took my hand.

After leading me back to the living room, he sat back down, his legs spread out, his arms stretched across the back of the couch, and that lust-filled gaze fixed on me. My nipples tightened, and I slowly crawled onto his lap.

Unsure. Nervous. Horny.

When my pussy brushed against his bulge, I sucked in another sharp breath and set my hands on his huge, rounded shoulders and relaxed on him. Last time that he had been inside me, he had stuffed an entire gallon of cum deep into my cunt.

And he was about to do it again.

Twice in one night.

For some godforsaken reason, I wanted it this time.

With one of his claws, he gently ripped the threads on my pants where the pant legs had been sewn together, creating a gaping hole near my entrance. I bit my lip and whimpered. How was this even real?!

I am about to fuck a sex demon. For the fourth time. Just this weekend.

He reached between us and pulled his huge cock out of his pants, resting it against his muscular abdomen. It extended to his sternum, his dick so wide that I could barely wrap both hands around it. There was no logical way that something this big could fit inside me.

But it had.

And it would again.

"I know it's too big for you," he murmured, swiping some hair off my forehead. "But we've made it fit before, and we'll make it fit into your tight little hole again. Okay?"

Warmth gushed between my thighs, and I clenched. "Yes."

Acaros lifted me with his hands on my waist. "Place your feet on the couch beside me."

I set the pads of my feet on the cushions beside his thighs, standing before him. Then, he pulled my hips down so I came down into a squat, the head of his cock at my entrance. My body rarely ever moved like this. I hated all things gym-related, especially squats.

But I could feel nothing but pleasure coursing through my body from this.

His eyes darkened, and he slammed me down on him, filling me up.

"Fuck!" I moaned, barely able to see straight.

"Grasp my horns."

I gently wrapped my hands around his horns.

"Harder," he groaned. "Use them to help you bounce up and down on my fat cock."

After grabbing his horns tighter, I used them to pull myself off his cock. Then, I dropped back down onto it, threw my head back, and screamed out in pleasure. With my eyes rolled back, I did it again and again and again.

Empty. Full. Empty. Full. Empty. Full.

"Oh my God," I cried.

"There's no God here, Hellcat," he groaned, lacing his hand through my hair and pulling my head back. "It's just you and a devil." He seized my hips and slammed up into me as I dropped down onto him. "No God could ever make you feel as good as I can."

Another moan left my mouth, my pussy tightening around him.

He sucked on my bare neck. "You drink my lust, and I drink yours."

"Always," I whispered, feeling his cock slide all the way up into my stomach.

"Faster."

I bounced on him faster, sweat rolling down my back and my heart pounding inside my chest, but the pleasure was far too good to stop. I curled my toes and continued, wanting to do nothing more than please him.

"Attagirl," he praised. "Look at how desperate you are for my cum."

I clenched tighter around him, my hands slipping from around his horns.

"Don't stop stroking those fucking horns."

I gripped his horns even tighter and glided my hands up and down them as I lifted myself up and slid back down, my pussy clinging on to every inch of his huge cock. Sweat rolled down my back, and I cried out in pleasure.

"Your belly is going to be full of my cum tonight."

"Fuck yes," I moaned, eyes rolling back.

"I'm going to dump so much of my cum into your holes that you'll never be able to wash it all out," he groaned against my bare neck. "You're going to have me inside you everywhere that you go."

My legs began trembling so hard that I could barely hold myself up, but I didn't stop.

I needed it. Badly.

"Come inside me," I cried, legs trembling. "P-p-please!"

He groaned softly. "Be careful what you beg for, Hellcat."

"Please!" I moaned, legs like Jell-O but still bouncing on him. "I need it."

"Fuck." He slammed into me and stilled. "Your pussy is mine." He pushed in another inch. "All mine." His balls pressed against my pussy. "My cum in your pussy is my claim on every inch of you." Somehow, when I thought he couldn't slide any deeper, he slammed into me deeper. "Mine."

CHAPTER
SIXTEEN

ACAROS

I LEANED against my bedroom doorframe, cock twitching inside my pants. Light flooded in through the windows.

With the blankets wrapped around her body, Iza slept in my Alaskan-king-size bed. While the mattress was just big enough for me in my demon form, the bed seemed to almost swallow Iza whole.

After sipping my cup of tea, I slipped out into the hallway and shut the door behind me.

Someone knocked on my front door, and I pulled the door open to see Qina standing in the hallway with her eyes a blazing red, mixed with green envy, and her arms crossed over her chest. "I heard that—"

Before she could say another word, I swung the door closed in her face.

What the fuck is she doing here? She knows not to show up to my place in Lust.

And I had never once told her about my high-rise in the city. She must've followed me or asked around The Lounge last night about where I had brought Iza. Hell … I didn't even remember seeing her there last night either.

"Acaros!" she shouted, banging louder on my door. "Open up!"

I glared at the door, my nails lengthening into claws and my nostrils flaring.

If she doesn't stop this shit, she'll wake Iza.

Another bang, and I swung the door open. "What the fuck are you doing here?"

"You brought another girl home. That's what—"

My hand snapped around her throat. I stepped out of my high-rise, shut the door behind me, and slammed her into the wall across from the door. "We're not a couple. We're not dating. I don't even fucking like you."

"Don't be like that, Ac—"

"Who sent you?" I asked between gritted teeth.

"Nobody," she said, squirming in my hold.

I tightened my grip so she couldn't move. "How'd you find my place?"

Her gaze tinted green. "An Envy can always find her way."

"You're half Envy, half succubus," I said, a growl clawing up the back of my throat. "You don't have that much power in either realm. So, I'm going to ask you again, Qina. Who sent you, and how'd you find out where I live?"

She pressed her lips together. "Why is there a human in your bed?"

"That's none of your fucking business."

"If I can't get it out of you, then I'll get it out of her."

"You touch a hair on her head, and I will suck the soul from your body." I hurled her toward the elevators and wiped my hand on my sweatpants, heading back toward my high-rise. "Don't fucking test me."

After walking back into my place and slamming the door, I picked up the teacup on the counter and sipped my hot drink, a low growl rumbling through me. Someone had given her my address and sent her to find me.

To pester me.

It could've been fucking anyone at The Lounge last night.

Like Amon. Or that flirty bartender. Or one of my best fucking friends.

A moment later, I listened as one set of feet padded out into the living room.

I gripped the teacup harder, vowing to figure out who it was once she left, and twisted my head around to see Iza walking toward me, dressed in one of my shirts that fell down past her knees and her hair a wild mess.

She looked down at my cup of tea and then giggled behind her hand.

"What?" I asked.

"Nothing," she said, though she didn't stop laughing.

I grabbed another teacup from the set. "Do you want some?"

"That's not it, but …" She quieted her giggles. "I'll have some."

After I poured her tea, I extended my arm for her to take the glass. When she reached for it, I pulled it a couple of inches away. "First, tell me why you're laughing. Did I do something to make you laugh?"

For two reasons …

One, because humans were strange creatures. I thought I had them all figured out, but sometimes, one—this one—surprised me by laughing at my tea. And, two, because I wanted her to laugh again. I liked the sound.

"It's just that your teacup doesn't fit the whole *scary demon* vibe."

"You're laughing at the size of my teacup?" I hummed, handing her the cup.

"More like the fact that you even own teacups." She brought the cup to her lips, paused, and sniffed it. "Wait. Does this have that weird lust potion, cum stuff inside it?" She pulled her lips away. "Because I can't do that so early in the morning."

My lips curled into a small smile, warmth spreading through my chest. "No."

What is this feeling? This warmth?

After shooting me a *I don't know if I believe you* look, she sipped the drink and walked over to the large windows that overlooked the city. I followed behind her, desperately wanting my hands all over her body again.

And again. And again. And again.

But I resisted the sweet, sweet temptation.

"I never thought I'd see the city from a view this beautiful," she whispered.

"Wait until you see my place in Lust."

She glanced over her shoulder at me. "What's Lust?"

"Lust is the kingdom in Hell where sex demons like me live ..." Though it was never my intention to mention it to her, never mind telling her that I wanted to bring her there. But the effect of this woman was stronger than any kind of Lust drug I'd ever taken.

An alarm rang from the phone in her purse that sat on the counter.

She furrowed her brows for a moment, then widened her eyes and slammed the boiling hot glass of tea into my chest, making a break for the door. "Oh my God. I'm going to be late for class." She swooped up her purse and twirled around, stumbling back to the door. "Thanks for the tea and for the, uh ... dick!"

I leaned back against the window with her tea running down my bare abdomen and watched her slam the door closed. Her scent lingered all over the apartment, her lust drifting through my nose.

While I wanted her to stay, I didn't think I would've had the control to hold myself back from pressing her up against the window and ravishing her for the rest of eternity. And I had to hold myself back.

Because I had work to do. People to find. And demons to kill.

All for Iza.

CHAPTER
SEVENTEEN

IZA

"DON'T FORGET that you have an exam next class," Professor Laufer said, standing in front of me and addressing the class. He knocked his knuckles on the table I sat at with Clayton and nodded to the class like he always did right before we left.

When other students began flooding out of the lecture hall, I spotted Mikayla and Jada at the door. Clayton glanced over at me nervously, adjusting his glasses.

He was a sweet kid, probably at the top of the class. Since I'd sat next to him in the beginning of the year, he had been acing every single quiz and exam that Professor Laufer had given us.

"Have you started studying yet?" Clayton asked me.

"No." I shoved my books into my backpack. "I've been ... *busy*."

"Party on Saturday night?" he asked with a small laugh.

I finished stuffing my books into my bag. "Something like that."

More like getting fucked by a huge sex demon from Hell, but a party worked too.

"If you wanna study together, I'll be in the library," he said. "Carltor Hall. Top floor."

"Thanks, Clayton," I said.

As he walked away nervously, I swung my backpack over my shoulder and glanced up at Professor Laufer, who was packing up his things at the front table, talking with a couple of students and looking at me.

My cheeks warmed, and I smiled at him, feeling ... the same way I had with Acaros.

It was the same sultry stare, the same mischievousness behind his smirk.

"See you later, Professor," I said, slipping out of the room.

"So?" Mikayla exclaimed immediately, shaking her head and impatiently waiting for me to talk about every little thing that had happened last night. She wrapped her hands around my upper arm and shook. "What happened with that demon?! Don't keep us waiting."

I shrugged my shoulders. "We just hung out."

"We want the details!" Mikayla said, pulling me to Smoothie Queen.

Jada arched her brow. "*Mikayla* wants the details."

When we reached the smoothie shop, we shuffled in line and ordered.

"I am *not* the only one!" Mikayla crossed her arms. "We've been making predictions all night about what he did with you. He was *soooo* much hotter than we'd expected him to be, and he's *huuuuuge*!"

Again, Jada snickered. "We saw that *thing* swinging last night ..."

"He's thick too," Mikayla said. "Your vagina must be aching."

My lips curled into a small smirk. "My vagina is doing fine. Don't worry."

"God, he's, like, seven feet tall," Jada commented.

"Almost nine with his horns."

"His horns?!" Mikayla exclaimed, smacking her hand over her heart. "I can't!"

I glanced over at her to see those curls half covering her over dramatic expression. "I am so glad that I could summon some *magic* for you on Halloween. No need to thank me for that huge—"

Jada elbowed her. "We need to get her a man before she combusts from excitement."

After picking up my smoothie from the counter, I slurped it and followed them to the exit of the building to the bus stop. Jada pushed some brown hair out of her face from the searing wind and brought her drink to her lips.

"There *has* to be others at our school, right?" Jada asked, glancing at Mikayla.

She sipped on her strawberry banana smoothie. "I don't know."

"Can't you sense them?" I asked.

"Who do you think I am?" she exclaimed.

"Well …" Jada cleared her throat. "Apparently some *powerful witch who demons fear.*"

Mikayla giggled. "Who told you that? Was it that guy you were flirting with last night?"

"You did!" Jada said.

Mikayla widened her eyes. "I did?"

Jada looked blankly at her. "What kind of shit is she on?"

"The good kind," I hummed, making the same joke that she had made Halloween night. I looped my thumbs around the straps of my backpack and continued toward the bus stop. "So, you don't know if there are others?"

"Demons?" Mikayla asked. "Not sure. But I'd bet there are, especially your professor."

"My professor?"

Mikayla grinned. "We saw the way he was staring at you."

"He was not."

Jada looped her arm around mine. "He totally was."

Mikayla mirrored her and looped her arm around my other arm. "You think he'll make your man jealous?"

"First of all, Acaros is not my man." I chewed on my inner cheek as jealousy pooled inside me. I balled my hands into fists. "I think he had a woman over this morning. A woman's shouting woke me up."

"You know what that means," Jada hummed, resting her head on my shoulder as we reached the bus stop. A line formed to ride the bus home. "You should make him jealous, like you did last night with that guy."

"I don't think that's smart."

"Who cares about smart?!" Mikayla said. "We want to make him jealous."

I arched a brow, warmth spreading through my body at how possessive he had become at The Lounge last night whenever that guy was talking to me. Ya girl was the complete opposite of petite, and that demon was nearly twice my size. But Acaros had tossed him like he weighed nothing to him.

The bus pulled to the corner, and I pulled out my student ID. After following the line up onto the bus, I tapped my student ID on the card reader and found an open seat toward the middle. Jada sat beside me, and Mikayla slouched behind us, leaning over our chair.

"You think I should make him jealous?" I asked.

"Hell yes!" Mikayla said, her red hair bouncing all over the place as the bus hit a pothole.

"And how do you think I should do that?"

Jada smirked. "First, don't go see him tonight."

Mikayla giggled wildly. "And second ... let's summon more sex demons tonight."

My eyes widened slightly. The thought of seeing Acaros a jealous and possessive mess because of this ... because of me ... made me warm in places that it shouldn't. I pressed my thighs together. What would Acaros do?

"Teasing a sex demon doesn't sound like a good idea." I smirked. "I'm in."

CHAPTER
EIGHTEEN

ACAROS

I KNOCKED BACK my Passion Delight and stared emptily at some succubi dancing around a pole, my mind only on Iza. My phone buzzed, and I turned it over to see another notification from Eros, asking me to take a summoning tonight.

He had been asking me since four in the afternoon, but I had no interest.

None. Zip. Zero.

I couldn't even find it in me to reply.

After I called the waiter over to grab another drink, Bazzon and Varoth walked into The Lounge and headed straight for our usual table. My phone buzzed again, and my gaze dropped to it, hoping that it was a notification from my security cameras back at home.

Iza had to show up tonight. Either at The Lounge or my house.

She had run out and left me completely flabbergasted when she thanked me for my dick. Nobody had done that before. Usually, succubi used me for my dick and left me in the early morning hours in a Lust Room.

But Iza had stayed all night.

"What's up?" Bazzon asked, slipping into the booth.

My teeth ground together. "Nothing."

Where the hell is she?

I looked up at the door, seeing two random women walk into the bar. *Fuck.*

Is she with another man? Maybe Qina said something to her to scare her away.

My gaze drifted to Qina, who sat at the bar, talking to a demon who had his back turned toward me, but she gave me her sultriest gaze, which had never done anything for me. My claws sank into my palms until they ripped apart my human skin.

"You good?" Bazzon asked.

"Fine," I growled, narrowing my glare.

Varoth sipped his drink. "You still thinking about that girl?"

"No."

Bazzon tipped his glass back. "Didn't see her for a few hours. Now, his dick's sad."

"Come on, dude." Varoth howled in laughter and nudged my shoulder. "Humans always crawl back to guys like us. Give her a day or so, and she'll be back, begging for your cock. Until then, why don't you find yourself a pretty lady? Qina keeps looking over here."

I cut my glare to him. "Did you send her?"

He scrunched his brows. "Did I send her where?"

"To my house this morning," I said. "I never told her where I live, but she showed up at my place. And if Iza had seen her, I would have had a mess to clean up." And I wasn't talking about Iza's feelings being hurt.

If Iza had seen Qina at my house and I saw her get teary-eyed, I would've killed Qina right then and there. I glared over at her, now chatting up Sawyer Laufer, who looked just as uninterested in her as I felt, thinking about her.

"Why would I send Qina to your place?" Varoth asked.

"Because you like Iza."

"I don't like Iza." He chuckled. "I don't fall for humans the way you do."

Bazzon squeezed my shoulder. "What happened to the player you used to be?"

"Get off me," I snarled, pissed that Iza was *nowhere* tonight.

"You're acting like Sawyer did ten years ago," Varoth said, sipping his drink. "All over that human girl, only for her to break his heart. It's a pity that asshole never recovered from that. Now, he's forced to chat up Qina just to get some pussy."

"You don't want to end up like him," Bazzon said.

"Sad life, not getting his dick sucked every night," Varoth commented.

I balled my hands into fists underneath the table and shoved my chair back. After downing the rest of my second Passion Delight of the night, I stormed over to Qina because I was certain that she had said something to Iza.

That, *and* I wanted to know who'd sent her.

Bazzon and Varoth were being too dickish right now.

"Hey, Acaros," Sawyer said.

"What did you do?" I growled at Qina.

Qina clicked her tongue, smiling at me. "Whatever do you mean?"

From a couple of chairs down, Dani and Eros both looked over at us. I cursed underneath my breath because I had wanted to avoid Eros *and* Dani tonight. A bouncer whispered something in Eros's ear, and then Eros slipped off his seat and headed over.

I seethed but kept myself together because I did *not* want to be kicked out of here, like they had promised to do last night when that asshole was hitting on my girl right in fucking front of me. So, I narrowed my gaze at Qina, warning her to speak.

"I didn't do anything." She crossed her arms. "Maybe Iza just doesn't like you."

My nostrils flared. "How do you know her name?"

She smirked and briefly looked back over at my friends. "Just heard it thrown around."

Eros whispered into Sawyer's ear, then found his way back to Dani. Dani slipped off her chair and dragged Eros back into a Lust

Room, throwing the waiter behind the bar a sultry smirk. Sawyer cleared his throat.

"I have to head out, but we should talk later, Acaros," Sawyer said. "It's important."

While Sawyer wasn't one of my immediate friends anymore, back in the day, we used to *share* a lot of things ... women included. But he had gotten away from the life of constant hookups a while ago after meeting one girl who ended up breaking his heart.

I had never understood it—or him—until now.

Until Iza.

"You know where to find me," I said, gaze fixed on Qina.

"Bye, Sawyer," Qina squeaked, waggling her fingers at him.

As Sawyer departed from The Lounge, I slammed my hand on the counter. "If I find out that you said anything to Iza to scare her away, we are going to have bigger problems than me sucking your soul and killing you."

"Like what?"

"Your sisters, dead. Your lineage, over." I stepped closer to her when she didn't react to the first two threats because I knew what would really get her. "And the crown that you're in line to inherit in Envy ... that crown will be Iza's."

CHAPTER
NINETEEN

IZA

WITH THE LIGHTS DIMMED, I sat in front of a Ouija board with Mikayla.

Jada walked in through the bedroom door and plopped down on her stomach, a bowl of popcorn in her hands. "We summon any shit yet?"

Mikayla had crystals scattered across my floor and sage burning from my nightstand, the smoke making my eyes teary. While sitting in a meditation position, she opened one eye. "It takes a long time. Patience."

Jada popped some popcorn into her mouth. "Ya know, I'm going to say it again. Demons might be real, but this magic that you're doing is definitely not." She snorted and kicked her legs back and forth. "Don't you think, Iza?"

I pressed my lips together as Mikayla cut her glare to me. "Of course not."

Once Mikayla looked away, I glanced toward Jada and snickered.

"Laugh all you want," Mikayla said, breathing in the sage. "You're getting fucked tonight."

"Oh, no." Jada giggled. "Definitely don't summon a guy with bulging muscles and a hu—"

"Shh!" Mikayla interrupted. "It's happening."

We waited and waited and waited. And nothing.

"I don't think—"

Thunder boomed overhead, and then the lights flickered. Warmth pooled in my stomach at the thought of Acaros showing up. We might've been summoning sex demons to make him jealous, but he'd show up, right?

"All right!" Mikayla leaped up from her seat and grabbed Jada's hand. "Now, come!"

Jada stumbled to her feet and grabbed the bowl, popcorn falling out of it all the way to the bedroom. "Where are we going?!" Jada said, mouth full of buttery popcorn. "I thought we were summoning sexy—"

"You gotta be in your bed for them to come."

"Oh my Lord," Jada said from the hallway, and I could just *hear* the eye roll in her voice.

Mikayla returned a moment later and slammed the door. "Have fun!"

I arched my brow and pushed up to my feet, immediately putting out the sage because it was going to put me in a goddamn coughing fit. Mikayla really had put on a whole production, hadn't she? Sage. Crystals. And a damn Ouija board.

After opening my window so the smoke would clear out of the room, I picked up the crystals that I'd kept stepping on with my bare feet and the popcorn. A cold breeze drifted into the room, and I shivered.

All I imagined was Acaros slipping through the open window, seizing my hips from behind, and having his way with me the way he had last night, and the night before, and the night before that.

But when I turned around, nobody was there. Only the curtains blowing into the room.

Maybe it didn't work this time.

So, I peeled off today's clothes and slipped into bed. Another crash of thunder rolled through the room, followed by lightning. And if I'd learned *anything* in science, lightning usually came first, didn't it?

Lightning flashed again, and suddenly, a figure appeared in front of the window, the moonlight eclipsed by his body.

"Iza," he said, voice floating through the air, deep but … different than Acaros's.

He stepped out of the light.

My eyes widened as I stared at Professor Laufer in front of me.

"What are you doing here?" I whispered, pulling the blankets to my chin.

"You summoned me."

"I—I … we … *fuck*."

A low chuckle escaped his mouth, and he stalked toward me until he reached the baseboard of my bed. He placed his hands on it, his veins prominent under the dim moonlight. "We won't be doing that tonight, Iza."

My mouth dropped open. "B-but you're … are you really a sex demon?"

"An incubus?" he asked. "Yes."

"Oh God," I muttered, running a hand through my hair. "I fucked up."

"By summoning demons after you've already been claimed by one? Yes, you have."

"You know?" I whispered.

"About Acaros? Yes. And he's fucking crazy about you."

My chest tightened, and guilt rushed through my body at the thought of betraying a man I barely knew. We had met only a couple of days ago, and I was so, so jealous of whoever that girl was who had been at his house this morning. For all I knew, it could've been his sister!

I sat up taller in my bed and drew my knees to my chest. "He is?"

"He's been looking for you all night. There are demons after you. *Following* you because of your relationship with him."

"Really?"

"Yes."

After scurrying out of the bed, I tugged on a pair of pants and ran a hand through my hair a couple of times to make it less of a mess. "Where is he?" I asked, grabbing my purse on my nightstand.

Before I could make it to the door, he grabbed my arm. "You're not going to find him."

"But—"

"If he knew that I was over here and let you leave in the middle of the night, neither of us would like the consequences." Professor Laufer released my arm and nudged me toward the bed. "He will find you tomorrow, but you need to rest because when he finds out that other demons have been summoned here tonight, you're going to get it."

My eyes widened. "I-I'm going to get it?"

A smirk crossed his face. "Yes."

With that, he turned on his heel, walked out of the bedroom, and shut my door behind him. I stared at the closed door through wide eyes and set down my purse on my nightstand, then spotted the light in Jada's room turn on through my window.

Suddenly, her shadow pressed up against the curtains, and then a man—a demon—much, much larger than Professor Laufer's human form, stepped behind her and seized her hips. I pulled my curtains shut to give them privacy and fell back on the bed, heart pounding.

Oh God ... I fucked up.

CHAPTER
TWENTY

IZA

I SAT in Professor Laufer's class with an exam in front of me, but my mind was freaking racing because of what he had told me last night. Acaros would find me. But when? Soon? After classes for the day? Would he return to my place?

And what the hell had he meant when he said that people were after me? Did Acaros know?

After peering up at Professor Laufer, who walked up and down the aisles with his arms crossed and his gaze on *me*, I stared through wide eyes at the exam. Why the hell was he looking at me like that?!

Suddenly, someone placed their hand on my shoulder from behind, and I jumped. Their other hand wrapped around the front of my mouth, and he pulled me to a standing position, his body pressed against mine.

"Hellcat, you're in trouble," Acaros growled into my ear. "Where were you last night?"

"I ... we—" My words were muffled. I glanced up at Professor Laufer, who still looked over.

Acaros pulled me out into the walkway and twirled me around, so I leaned against the edge of the desk and stared up at him, his hand still on my mouth. My eyes widened even more, and I nervously glanced around because he was in his demon form!

Could ... could people see us?

All the students were still completing their exams, and nobody had looked over. Yet.

"There's a demon in this class," Acaros said, "who has been following you around."

My eyes widened. The only person who had done that was *him*!

"Trying to take you from me," he growled, scanning the room with blazing eyes.

"Acaros," I whispered against his hand, "could it be Prof—"

Before I could finish my sentence, Acaros twirled me around again and picked me right up into the air, my back against his huge chest and his arms wrapped underneath my legs. My skirt bunched up by my hips, giving the class a view of my panties.

"Acaros!" I whisper-yelled.

"Remember what I told you last time, Hellcat. If you yell, they'll hear you. *See you.*"

But how would he find who was after me? Or maybe ... this was my punishment for not coming to see him last night. But I mean, come on; he could've come to see me, but he hadn't. Instead, I had been jump-scared by Laufer.

"Only demons can see us," he said, ripping off my underwear and dropping them in the middle of the walkway. He positioned himself at my entrance. "I'll kill whoever's ass who looks up to watch me fuck you."

My eyes widened, and I glanced over at Professor Laufer.

While I wanted to tell him that it was Professor Laufer—that it had to be because I had seen him last night—if I said a word, then someone would hear me. But even if I wanted to, Acaros gave me *no* warning before plunging right into me.

Body shaking in pleasure, I bit down on my lip to muffle a scream.

Nobody looked up.

He slammed into me harder, and I slapped a hand over my mouth. "Acaros ..."

"Students," Professor Laufer said.

My eyes widened as all the students looked up at him in the front of the class. We stood feet from Professor Laufer, right in the goddamn front, while Acaros literally rammed his fat cock into me over and over, scanning the room like a psychopath.

As if he had already found the culprit that he apparently thought was stalking me, he growled into my ear and walked right toward the sweet, nerdy Clayton, who was gripping his pencil hard in his hand and staring softly up at Professor Laufer.

"Acaros," I whispered, completely useless in his arms, "it's not Clayton!"

"Let's pull these nice, round tits out, and we'll see," he murmured into my ear, his talons curling around the neckline of my shirt and pulling it down so my breasts fell out of my shirt and bra, on display for everyone to see *if they could*. "An incubus won't be able to resist tits like this."

The class still stared at Professor Laufer, who, for some goddamn reason, seemed to be working *with* Acaros! Acaros bounced me up and down on his cock, my tits moving like crazy and my pussy on full display to anyone who dared to look.

"Hold on," Acaros whispered into my ear.

Hold on? Hold on to what?

My eyes widened, and suddenly, Acaros dropped me forward. I reached behind me and grabbed each of his shoulders, my tits hanging in front of me, bouncing inches above Clayton's desk and centimeters from his face.

Each time Acaros thrust into me, my tits bounced closer to his mouth.

"Fucker is hard," Acaros snarled behind me.

Clayton moved his hand over his crotch to cover his dick, but I had seen it. His cock was throbbing against his jeans. My eyes widened, and I sucked in a sharp breath, clenching around Acaros.

Clayton furrowed his brows together and glanced over at my tits, then up at me.

"I just want a taste," he mumbled.

When he reached forward, Acaros snapped me back toward him. "You want a taste?"

Eyes glazed over with lust, he nodded. "Just one."

Acaros chuckled darkly behind me. After a couple more grunts, he lifted me into the air again, my back against his chest and his strong arms underneath my legs. He walked to the edge of Clayton's desk and held me over it. One more thrust up into me, and he growled into my ear, both of us being sent over the edge.

I gripped his arms, my entire body shaking, and bit my lip to keep myself quiet.

But fuuuuuuuck!

"You're mine," Acaros snarled into my ear. "And we're going to show him."

"Wh-what?" I whispered, head in a daze.

The more and more cum that he pumped into my pussy, the more that I could feel ... slowly slipping out of me, running down my thighs, and dripping all over Clayton's exam. My eyes widened, and I tried to reach down to cover my cunt, but Acaros stopped me.

"You're mine," he repeated, voice rougher. "Mine."

"B-but—"

"He'll lick it up like the dirty, desperate dog he is," he said. "You're mine."

He slammed deeper into me, making more spill out.

"Mine."

He thrust into me again.

"Mine."

So much cum had spilled out of me and onto the desk that it began dripping off the sides and onto Clayton's dick that he had pulled out of his pants. The head of his cock was coated in a thick layer of cum, rolling down his shaft.

I tightened around Acaros, forcing more out of me.

Clayton grunted and wrapped his hand around his cock.

My heart pounded inside my chest, and I curled my toes, clenching again.

Fuck, why is this so hot?

"That's the only bit of my girl that you'll ever get," Acaros growled, pulling his cock out of my pussy and letting the rest of our cum drip out of me. He hovered me over the desk, coating every inch of it in cum, marking his territory. "Savor it while you can."

CHAPTER
TWENTY-ONE

IZA

"YOU CAN HAND in your exams up front," Professor Laufer said to the class.

My eyes widened as I still sat helplessly in Acaros's hold, the cum drooling out of my pussy and onto Clayton's desk. After lolling my head back against his shoulder, I tried to pull my legs together, but he wouldn't let me.

Clayton scooped up some cum on his fingers and stuffed it into his mouth.

"You're lucky I don't make *you* clean up your mess," Acaros growled into my ear.

When my pussy tightened at the sound of his voice, more cum dripped out of me.

Students began walking down the stairs toward the front of the class to hand in their exams, passing us like we weren't even there. When the doors opened up top, a gust of cold air rolled down the auditorium and hit my cunt.

I whined softly and knit my brows together.

"Where were you last night?" Acaros asked, fingers circling my clit.

"At home," I whispered.

His fingers moved faster. "What were you doing?"

After swallowing hard, I tilted my head on his shoulder and looked at the sharp features of his face and those goddamn huge horns. Now wasn't the time to think dirty thoughts, but it sure was better than telling him that we had tried to summon another sex demon.

"What. Were. You. Doing?" he growled. "Don't make me repeat myself again."

"We were ... having a good time," I whispered, biting back a moan.

He massaged my clit faster and faster, teetering me on the edge. "How?"

"By the sound of it," I said, "you already know what I was doing."

A couple more moments passed of him furiously rubbing my clit, and all of the students, except Clayton, had turned in their exams and left. Clayton, on the other hand, was stuffing fingers' worth of cum into his mouth.

Once all the cum disappeared off Clayton's desk, he sat back in his chair with his entire eyes—the whites and all—turned a hazy black. He licked his lips with a forked tongue and twisted them into a small smirk. "You taste so good."

"You have some explaining to do tonight," Acaros said into my ear.

For a second time, Clayton moved toward me. "I want more ... more ..."

Before he could touch me, Acaros set me down on shaky legs and snapped his hand around Clayton's throat. With wide eyes, I stared at Acaros dragging Clayton out of the classroom. No, not through the doorway, but directly through one of the windows toward the side. Professor Laufer clicked his tongue while he leaned against his desk.

He extended his suit jacket that had been slung against the back of his seat. "Here."

I shrugged it over my shoulders and buttoned it all the way up because for some reason, everyone in this damn university was a sex demon, apparently! And I didn't want anyone to get the wrong idea. Especially Acaros.

Professor Laufer cleared his throat and stared at the broken window. "So, how's Jada?"

Eyes widening, I glanced over at him. "Why?"

After holding my stare for a couple of moments, he shuffled some papers together. Mid-shuffle, he sniffed the air, looked toward the open door, where she and Mikayla peered into the room, and stiffened.

While Jada usually had her shit together, she stood in the middle of the doorway, her nipples taut against the front of her shirt and her eyes wide.

Mikayla glanced between them, her smirk widening as she mouthed, *I fucking knew it!*

"There's too many fucking people around here," Acaros said suddenly, throwing Clayton back into the room and dragging him halfway down the staircase. He dropped him and muttered a couple of words, black mist forming in front of him.

Clayton lay at Acaros's feet, wearing cracked glasses with two hazy black eyes. "I want more." He looked up at me. "More. Give me more, Iza. I want more of you." He scrambled to his knees and began taking off toward me. "More. I need more!"

Before he could get halfway down the steps, Acaros seized him. Gusts of wind blew from what looked to be a portal into the auditorium, blowing back my curls. I followed Acaros back up the steps.

"Where are you taking him?" I asked.

"To Hell."

"To Hell?!"

"I'll be back in ten minutes," he said. "Don't go anywhere."

"But—"

After growling, Acaros turned toward me. "I will deal with *you* when I return."

And with that, he disappeared through the portal. I stared in surprise at the black mist spinning in circles in front of me, then looked over my shoulder to see Professor Laufer still staring up at Jada.

Welp ...

While I wasn't one for doing anything crazy—really, I wasn't that kind of girl—Acaros had a special kind of hold on me. So, before Professor Laufer or my friends could stop me, my ass stepped right into the portal just as it was disappearing.

CHAPTER
TWENTY-TWO

IZA

AFTER STUMBLING FORWARD into the portal, I blinked my eyes a couple of times. Blurry objects blazed through my vision, hazy memories were fuzzy in my mind, and the whispers of demons drifted through my ears.

When I finally regained my eyesight, I looked around to find Acaros, but instead, I saw …

Demons.

Demons everywhere.

"WHAT THE FUCK?!" I screamed at the top of my lungs. "Get away from me!"

I turned around in an attempt to hurry back into the classroom, to get back to my life and to my friends because this was a mistake. A huge mistake. What had possessed me to follow Acaros through the portal? Maybe jealousy that he would see someone else down here?

When one touched my thigh, I screamed again and kicked them hard in the balls. No matter what way I looked, I was surrounded by darkness and hungry shadow-like demons heading my way.

The portal had disappeared completely. And I was stuck.

My mouth dried, and I shuffled backward, only to hit another demon, who wrapped his hands around my upper arms. Before I knew it, hands were all over my body, touching me, groping me, fondling me in places that only Acaros had.

"Acaros!" I screamed, hoping that he'd hear me. "Please!"

"Move!" a female shouted to my left.

Then a small hand wrapped around my wrist and yanked me forward. I screamed as I fell and I fell and I fell. My arms and legs flailed around while I desperately tried to catch my footing.

Suddenly, a soft pink light appeared ahead of me, and within a moment, I dropped into a room. I landed with a thud in front of another large, misty black portal and grunted. I didn't believe in a god, but, damn, was I thanking one right about now ...

"Iza," a female said.

I peered up to see that girl from The Lounge the other night. She stood in a fairly large room with egg-white walls and two red velvet couches on either side of the portal. Two guards, dressed in suits with reflective black eyes and huge horns, stood beside her under the dim light.

"I'm Dani. We met at The Lounge," Dani said. "You're safe here."

While Dani was sweet, I had just walked through literal Hell with demons everywhere, and I might or might not have been freaking out a little bit. I looked over my shoulder and chewed on my inner cheek, really making sure that I was okay.

"Thank you," I whispered.

"What are you doing here?" Dani asked, brows furrowed. "How'd you find this place?"

I opened and closed my mouth a handful of times. "I ... we ... Acaros ..."

She arched a brow. "What'd Acaros do?"

"I followed him into a portal," I whispered. "I'm sorry. I just want to go home."

"Nonsense," she said. "You're already here. Let's get you fed."

While it probably wasn't that smart to eat in Hell—*because what did they eat, human flesh?!*—I followed Dani out the double doors and stopped. The sky was a light pink with feathery white clouds. Beds of roses lined the white stone walkways, which led to a towering castle.

Dani giggled and pressed two fingers against my chin to close my open mouth. "You don't want to keep your mouth open like that for too long or else the flying dicks might find you and use you for eternity."

My mouth dropped open even more. "There're flying dicks?!"

Another laugh left her mouth. "To the northeast. There is an entire island of them."

I looked over at her, eyes so wide that I thought I popped a blood vessel. "You're lying."

"I can bring you there if you—"

"No!" I exclaimed. "I need to rest after that portal."

And besides, if Acaros found out that I'd summoned another sex demon last night, followed him into a portal because I had no self-control, then visited an island with flying dicks, I didn't know *what* he would do to me.

"You're lucky that I was returning home at just the right time," she said. "You could've been stuck in that portal for days. Or worse ... I heard that someone had it out for you. If they'd found you first, then ..."

My eyes widened even more. "Then what?"

She pressed her lips together and stayed quiet, and I decided to drop it. Acaros and Professor Laufer had mentioned that someone had it out for me because I was dating—*are we dating?*—Acaros, and I could only imagine what would happen.

After looping her arm around mine, she guided me toward another walkway off the main one. Demons walked to and from the nearest bustling town, their eyes hazy with lust and pink drinks in their hands.

"That town is called Chastion," Dani said. "I'm sure Acaros will take you there sometime."

"I don't know about that."

"Why?"

"He's kinda mad right now."

"At you?"

"Maybe?" I squeaked. "My friends and I—mostly my friends—summoned a demon last night, and it wasn't him. He swooped into my classroom and basically fucked me in front of everyone without them knowing, and now, I'm here."

She burst out into laughter. "Sounds like you had quite the day. I'm jealous."

My lips curled into a small smile, and I found myself laughing along with her. I didn't know her true intentions, nor why she'd invited me to dinner and not sent me off through the portal back home. But something about her felt safe.

"Dani!" a woman called to our right. "Over here!"

"Come," Dani said, grabbing my hand and leading me toward a garden, where a woman who looked similar to Jada stood with a picnic basket. "I've asked one of my maids to set up a dinner for us in the Garden of Passion."

But if Dani had asked for her maid to set out a dinner for us, then she must've known that I would be here. Yet my trip to Hell hadn't been planned at all, more of a spur-of-the-moment kind of decision. So, how had she known that I'd show up in Hell?

CHAPTER
TWENTY-THREE

IZA

"SO, HOW'D YOU LIKE IT?" Dani asked with a grin.

Through wide eyes, I stared at the foyer to her castle that we had just toured. I couldn't even count how many rooms there were on each floor, nor could I remember how many floors there were. Everything was more exquisite than *anything* I had seen on Earth.

"There's still more," Dani said, looping my arm around hers and tugging me along.

"More?!" I exclaimed. "How can there be any more?"

"I've been gatekeeping my favorite part." She giggled. "The Lust Rooms."

My eyes widened. "The Lust Rooms? What are those?"

"Where demons fulfill their every desire." She pulled me down a set of steps and toward a large hallway filled with ten-foot-tall doors that were wider than my arm span. "I'm surprised that Acaros hasn't brought you to them yet. They have some at The Lounge."

Chest tightening, I sucked on my inner cheek. Was that why he hung out there? Did he bring other girls into Lust Rooms? Maybe that woman who was at his place the other morning ... I thought she had been at The Lounge the other night too.

"Follow me into the first—"

"Iza!" someone shouted from behind me.

I twirled around to see Acaros storming our way in his demon form, his brows furrowed together and a pissed-off glare branded onto his face.

When he finally made it to me, he grabbed my hand and pulled me behind him. "What are you doing with her?"

"I'm just showing her around the Lust Rooms," Dani said.

"Why?" he gritted through clenched teeth, his grip tightening. "She's mine."

Light danced in Dani's eyes. "Then, why haven't you brought her to a Lust Room?"

Acaros dug his claws into my waist. "Stay away from her."

"Is that any way to talk to your queen?" Dani hummed.

"If she's trying to steal your girl, yes."

His girl ...

There it was again. He had said it to Clayton earlier after I came all over his desk, telling him to savor every last bit of me because that was the only taste that Clayton would ever get from *his girl*. And now ... he was telling Dani almost the same thing.

"I'm not trying to steal your girl," Dani said. "I'm just showing her what she's missing because *you* haven't brought her here for me to officially meet her and *you* let her stumble through the portal by herself. Do you know how terrifying that is for a human?"

Instead of responding to her, Acaros turned us around and marched us all the way out of the castle. I stumbled onto the white walkway toward Chastion and looked over my shoulder to see Dani smirking and waving me off.

After a couple of moments, Acaros released his harsh grip on me. "I'm sorry."

"What?" I asked, taken aback and looking up at him.

"I'm sorry," he repeated.

"For what?"

"I had to take care of that prick," he said through gritted teeth. "And I left you alone."

"It's okay. But where did you take Clayton?"

After a low growl, he cut his eyes to me. "Don't worry about it."

"Did you kill him?"

"No."

I crossed my arms. "Why don't I believe that?"

"He's in Wrath."

"What's Wrath?"

"Wrath is a kingdom of lava in Hell where demons reside. I brought him to the torture—"

"You're torturing him?!" I exclaimed. "But he's so sweet."

"He wanted to fuck you."

"So, you're going to throw everyone who has ever wanted to fuck me in some torture pits?!" I asked, throwing my hands up. When he didn't react, I re-crossed my arms and looked toward the garden. "Besides, you can't do that. There are not enough pits to hold all the men—"

"Don't finish that fucking sentence," he growled. "Who are they?"

"Wouldn't you like to know?"

"Yes, I would." He snapped his hand around my elbow. "Now."

"That is none of your business."

"You *are* my fucking business, Iza. First, I had to hear from Laufer that *you* had summoned a sex demon last night. Next, you wandered into the portal after I explicitly told you to stay on Earth. Then, I found you in a Lust Room with Dani, the commander of Lust and one of the most *influential* demons."

"Well"—I chewed on my lip—"you see, I can explain all that, quite logically even."

"You'd better start," he growled. "Why'd you summon a demon last night?"

"Because ..."

"*Because* doesn't cut it, Hellcat."

"Because I wanted to get you jealous," I whispered. "The way that you made me."

"What are you talking about?"

"That girl who was at your place the other morning. Ring a bell?"

"Qina?"

"Qina," I repeated, her name sour on my tongue. "She was shouting at you."

And I hadn't known if it was an angry shout or one of pleasure. He was so good when we were together that I could only imagine him touching another girl the way that he touched me, making her scream and shout how I had so many times now.

"Don't worry about her."

Says every guilty guy ever.

"Why was she over at your house?" I asked.

"Because someone had sent her."

"Why was she screaming?"

"Because she didn't like that I didn't want her there."

"Well then, why haven't you brought me into a Lust Room?" I asked.

"You want to know why I haven't brought you into a Lust Room?"

I glared up at him. "Mmhmm."

Within a moment, Acaros twirled me around and bent me over the fence to the garden. Right in the middle of the walkway to Chastion. Right in the center of people heading to and from the castle.

"Acaros," I hissed, "what are you—"

Before I could finish my sentence, he slipped his cock under my skirt and pressed the head against my cunt. My eyes widened, and I attempted to stand back up because we were literally in front of everyone! But he held me in place and slammed into me.

"This is why I haven't brought you to a Lust Room," he grunted. "It's too private, and I love the way your pussy tightens around my cock when we're in public, when you have a fear of being caught."

CHAPTER
TWENTY-FOUR

ACAROS

WHEN I SLAMMED my dick all the way into her cunt, I grunted and wrapped an arm around her throat, my biceps against her neck, not tightly, but enough to hold her in place. Her pussy became even wetter around me.

My lips curled into a smirk against her ear. "Guess what."

She glanced around and tried squirming out of my hold again, but I wasn't going to let her go. Not now. Not when she was a jealous wreck, thinking that I'd wanted Qina to come over, thinking that was the reason I hadn't brought her to a Lust Room yet.

"Everyone is staring at us," she whispered.

"That's because everyone in Lust can see me pounding into your tight little pussy."

"Acaros," she whispered, cheeks now flushing, "we need to—"

"Give them a show," I said, slamming into her and making her tits bounce out of her little tank top. I thrust into her again, her breasts continuing to bounce against my arm. "Show them what they're missing out on by hiding in those Lust Rooms to fuck."

While she clawed at my forearm with those dainty, dull finger-nails, she moaned and tightened around me. I slammed into her again, only to listen to all those little whimpers she tried to keep hidden.

"You love this, don't you?" I asked.

"No."

I picked up one of her legs into the air, giving everyone a view of her cunt. "You sure about that, Hellcat? All your cunt has been doing since I plunged into you is tightening around my fat cock." My lips curled into a smirk. "And you haven't asked me to stop."

"S-s—" she started, eyes rolling back. "Don't stop."

A satisfied groan left my throat. "Beg me not to stop."

Her entire body tightened in my hold as she looked around at the onlookers beginning to form around us. Lust demons weren't going to miss a show as good as this one—a human in Lust being used by one of the biggest demons around.

I grabbed her hand and placed it over her belly. "Beg for me to keep pounding into you this deep so everyone can watch."

"Please keep fucking me," she begged. "Please!"

"More."

"Please keep fucking me so …" she cried. "So …"

"So, what, Hellcat?"

"So we can give everyone a show!" she screamed.

After tightening my arm around her throat, I slammed into her harder and faster. My cock was buried so deep inside her that every time I thrust up, she could feel *and see* it in her stomach, as could everyone else.

"You don't know how much I love fucking you like this," I growled into her ear. "Letting everyone see your pretty pussy as I thrust into it, the way it quivers around my dick right before you're about to explode."

A low groan escaped through my teeth, and I picked her up right off the ground. I didn't care how many times we did it in this position in front of everyone; I would never get fucking tired of it. I loved the way it felt when she couldn't hold all my cum inside her, when it began pouring out of her pussy because it was too tight.

"Fuck, Hellcat," I growled. "Keep moaning."

She rested her head against my shoulder and cried out in pleasure. "Acaros."

"Just like that. Just fucking like that."

She rolled her head from side to side on my shoulder, her entire body tensing. A large group of demons had formed around us, watching my pretty little human whimper and whine because of me.

"Please, don't stop," she cried. "Keep fucking me."

"Louder."

"Please! Give me your cum. I need it!"

"Are you going to be a good girl and hold it all inside yourself this time?" I asked, knowing that she would never be able to hold it all inside her. I had too much of it that I kept filling her pussy with. Even if she could, her pussy was full from earlier today in the classroom.

"Yes!" she cried. "Yes! I'll keep it all in my pussy. I promise."

"What happens if you break your promise to me?" I asked, steadily pumping into her.

"I won't."

"But what if you do?"

"I'll—I'll … I'll be your dirty little slut for the rest of eternity."

Holy fuck!

Before she could speak another word, I slammed into her as quickly and as deeply as I could. She would never be able to keep her end of the deal, and she hadn't even known that she was making a deal with a demon.

A deal that would bind her to me forever.

And there was no way in fucking hell that I would pass up on this.

"Are you ready?" I asked, giving her every chance to keep her promise.

"Give it to me!" she cried, throwing her head back against my shoulder. "Please!"

I slammed into her as deeply as I could, my cum pumping past her cervix for a second time today. Her entire body trembled uncontrollably, her eyes rolling back in her head. I held her steady and could already begin to feel the thick cum rolling down my dick and balls, dripping onto the walkway underneath us.

After a few more final pumps, I slowly pulled out of her pulsing cunt. When my dick fell out of her and slapped against my thigh, my cum began running down her thighs—her promise broken and our deal final.

Complete.

She was mine. For eternity.

"You break promises quite quickly," I hummed in amusement.

"Hmm?" she asked, looking up at me. Then, her eyes widened and dropped to her legs. She placed both her hands on her cunt to hold the cum inside her as everyone slowly dispersed around us. "Wh-what am I going to do?"

My cum drooled around her fingers and dripped onto the white walkway to Chastion.

I grabbed her hand, not caring that it was covered in my cum, and tugged her toward the town. "You're going to let my cum run down each of your thighs and leave a trail of my cum all the way back to my place."

"Acaros!"

When I snatched up her other hand to lift it into the air, her skirt rose on her thighs. "Fuck, Hellcat, you look so pretty with my cum all over you like that." My dick stiffened. "You don't know what you do to me."

"B-but what if someone sees?" she squeaked, suddenly self-conscious even though tons of demons had just watched me fuck her.

"Even better." I eyed her thick thighs. "They'll know you're mine."

She pressed them together, making more cum ooze between the crevices.

Fuck.

A low growl escaped my throat. "I want to fucking cover you in my cum."

Head to fucking toe. I wanted her drenched and licking it up from every part of her body. Like a cute little innocent toy that I could play with all day, every day, until she couldn't go an hour without more. Until she begged me to fill her.

And now, I could. She'd promised herself to me. For eternity.

CHAPTER
TWENTY-FIVE

IZA

AFTER TREKKING through Chastion with cum drooling down my thighs, I waddled up a set of house steps in the city center. For our entire walk back to Acaros's place, Acaros seemed ... different. More confident, cocky even.

As soon as I stepped into Acaros's house, unfamiliar sensations shot through my system. Shadows and dark ethereal lights in the front room danced on the dark stone walls as a source of light, casting mesmerizing patterns on the furniture.

Talk about this place being wildly different from his apartment on Earth.

On Earth, his high-rise had a broody billionaire vibe to it. *This* felt like a demon space.

I continued to walk through the house, the air charged with an alluring energy and the scent of incense that did all sorts of terrible things to my ... pussy. The wetness between my thighs seemed to only grow.

After calming myself—as much as I could—I grazed my fingers across the fallen-angel sculptures that adorned the corner of the living room, representing creatures that I had once only thought were mythological.

A plush obsidian-black velvet couch lay in the center of the living room, adorned with crimson throw pillows that seemed to pulsate. Yes, pulsate. Like a damn vibrator. And I couldn't stop freaking thinking about getting myself off on it while Acaros watched.

But … I needed to get this cum off my thighs first. Or else I'd stain his house with it.

"Do you have a bathroom?" I asked, glancing over at him. "To wipe all this cu—"

When my gaze locked on to the bookshelf built into the wall behind Acaros, I widened my eyes. I walked over to them and drew my fingers over the spines of the books—which looked like actual human spines. Unable to help myself, I pulled one out.

The book was written in a language that I couldn't read—probably some form of demon—and had been sitting alongside ancient spell books, one that looked similar to a book that Mikayla had at our place.

"How do you like it?" Acaros asked.

"It's amazing," I whispered.

"Good, because you're going to live the rest of your life here."

I snapped my gaze to him. "What?"

He popped open the fridge in the next room and pulled out two beer bottles that had a pink label, reading *Your Favorite Passion Delight.* "You heard me," he said, handing me one of the bottles and dropping it as if that explained everything.

"What are you talking about?" I pushed.

"You promised yourself to me."

Still, what the hell was he talking about?! I didn't remember—

Fuck.

"That was in the heat of the moment," I whispered, heart pounding. "I didn't mean—"

Acaros stalked toward me, his gaze low and dark. "Ah, it doesn't matter what you meant. You made a promise to me. You sold your soul to a demon. And I don't plan on letting you take back anything."

When he reached me, my gaze focused on his stomach in front of me. Then, I craned my head up to see his entire form looming over me. A sinister smirk was painted on his lips, which I imagined all over me.

While I had always known that he was huge, somehow, his presence here felt more than welcoming, less scary. I swallowed hard and held myself back from climbing up that man and telling him that I didn't care I had sold my soul to him.

"You're mine now," he said, capturing my chin in his hand. "Say it."

"Yours," I whispered.

"*Say it.*"

"I'm yours now."

"For eternity."

"For eternity."

"Good," Acaros said.

Then, in one swoop, he tossed me over his shoulder and headed through the house and up the steps. Candlelight flickered on the walls to a room at the end of a hallway. Acaros set me down, and I blinked a couple of times to regain my composure from being so close to him.

We stood in his bedroom, which looked to be carved out of the house's obsidian stone. Midnight-colored drapes hung beside the windows, letting in the soft-colored light from outside. I moved toward the bed and drew my fingers across the eerily elegant silk bedding.

Acaros disappeared into a connected room, then returned a moment later with a towel.

Instead of tossing me around like he usually did, Acaros dropped to his knees in front of me and tapped on my shin so I'd part my legs. When I did, he placed the warm and wet towel on my thighs, wiping away any trace of his cum.

My eyes widened slightly, seeing him so … soft.

The night I'd met him, he had been so hard, so uncaring. And now, he was on his knees in front of me, cleaning me off instead of forcing me to do it myself. Warmth spread through my chest, making me tingle all over my body.

Once he finished, he returned the towel to the bathroom. I sat on the bed, heart pounding. While I had lain in his bed before and fallen asleep with him, I didn't know what a night in Hell would be like.

Acaros crawled into the bed and wrapped his hands underneath my arms to pull me back with him. I lay with my back on his chest and my gaze focused on the black wall across from us.

"Are we going to have sex?" I whispered.

A low chuckle came from his throat. "If I fuck you for a third time today, you'll break."

"I will not! What do you think I am?" I exclaimed.

"A weak human."

After turning in his arms, I cuddled closer to him and placed my legs over his. "I am not."

He wrapped his arms around my torso and pulled me closer. "You don't think so?"

"Nope."

His features softened. "Oh yeah?"

"Yep."

Instead of responding with something slick, he smiled. Yes, smiled. Not one of his smirks. And it was one of the prettiest things I had ever seen. He tucked some hair behind my ear and tilted his head to the side, just a couple of centimeters.

"I think I understand how Sawyer felt," he whispered.

My brows furrowed. "Who's Sawyer?"

He smiled a bit more, a dimple forming on his left cheek. "Don't worry about it, Hellcat."

CHAPTER
TWENTY-SIX

ACAROS

SHADOWS DANCED on the curtains like whispers from all the demons returning home after spending the night in Lust Rooms. I stood at the foot of the bed with my hands on the footboard, gripping it tightly to keep myself in control.

The first rays of pink sunlight drifted into the room, illuminating Iza's dark skin. I bit back a growl, not wanting to break her, but the *lust* was too heavy to handle. I had been up for two hours, my dick rock fucking hard and her pretty pussy smelling like I needed to eat it.

I wrapped my hand around the base of my cock and growled. "Stop it, Acaros."

If I fucked her again, I'd break her. And she needed to last for eternity with me.

A soft pink halo seemed to wrap around her body, accentuating the soft curves of her face … and her tits, which were spilling out from underneath the blankets. I dropped my gaze and focused on the black footboard, nearly splitting it into two pieces.

"Fuck," I whispered. My dick hurt.

After deciding to move closer—I wouldn't touch her; I just

wanted a better view of her—I sat on the edge of the bed with one hand still on my cock. I brushed a strand of curls away from her face, my fingertips on fire as soon as they touched her skin.

My gaze dropped down to her round tits, and I gripped my dick harder. Once I gently pulled back the blankets, revealing her sexy body, I moved my hand up and down my cock. Slowly at first.

But then ... I couldn't help myself any longer.

One taste wouldn't hurt, right?

I parted her legs and dipped my hand between them, dick twitching in my hand. My fingers disappeared between her pussy lips, rubbing that sensitive bud and dropping even lower to her wet cunt.

When they were covered in her juices, I sucked them into my mouth.

One taste ...

One more *taste.*

I crawled between her legs, trailed my nose up her inner thigh, savoring the sweet scent of her pussy for me, and placed my lips on her lips, licking up what I could of her juices because I couldn't get enough of her.

"Your pussy tastes so good."

She couldn't hear me, but it didn't matter. I wanted more. I *needed* more.

After placing my lips around her clit, I sucked it gently into my mouth and drew my tongue back and forth around it. She stirred underneath me, but didn't awaken, the lust pouring out of her pussy.

I gripped her thighs and pulled her closer to me.

Hungry.

So hungry.

When I couldn't handle just grinding myself into the mattress anymore, I lifted my head from her pussy. Her juices ran down my chin. She whimpered softly, her pussy clenching and unclenching. Practically begging for me.

"Sorry, Hellcat," I mumbled, crawling up the bed and climbing between her legs. I positioned my cock at her entrance, my pre-cum dripping onto her pretty lips. "I can't help myself around you." And with that, I pushed myself inside her and grunted.

Her warm pussy tightened around my cock, gripping me at the base and all the way down to the tip every time I pulled out of her. I gripped her shoulders and moved further up the bed to get deeper inside her.

"Look what you do to me," I whispered into her ear.

"Acaros," she moaned softly.

"Sorry if I woke you, Hellcat," I murmured, placing my lips on her forehead and still pumping into her.

She arched her back and shifted in the bed, spreading her legs a bit wider to give me easier access. I gripped her shoulders faster and pounded into her tight cunt, her tits bouncing against my chest and making my balls feel heavier.

"Acaros!" she cried. "I'm going to come."

"Already, Hellcat? I just started."

Her body began trembling around me, pulsing on my cock. I cocked my head back and groaned in pleasure as she milked every last drop of my cum out of my balls. And yet I continued to pump into her to push it deeper.

Yesterday, she'd tried to push back that she didn't want to stay here with me forever. So, like I had promised, I would do anything to get her pregnant with *my* child so she couldn't leave me. So we would be bonded forever.

CHAPTER
TWENTY-SEVEN

IZA

"SO, HOW WAS IT?" Mikayla asked, walking with me to The Lounge bar the next night.

My lips curled into a small smile, heat burning my cheeks. "It was good."

She nudged me. "Just good?"

"I can't explain my entire sex life to you!" I exclaimed. "It's private ..."

And embarrassing because *how* could I tell her that after my curious ass had stepped through that portal to follow Acaros, he'd fucked me in the middle of the walkway and forced me to do my own little walk of shame back to his house?

Mikayla giggled. "Well, if you'd like to know, Jada and Sawyer are getting along nicely."

"Sawyer?"

After wrapping an arm around my shoulders, Mikayla turned me around and pointed halfway across the bar, where Jada sat with Professor Laufer. Was Sawyer his first name? Hadn't Acaros said it last night? Something about knowing what he felt like? What had that meant?

"They've been together, fucking, all night," Mikayla said. "I heard it through the walls."

I stifled a laugh. "I bet you had a blast, listening to her moan."

Mikayla rolled her eyes playfully. "Actually, I had someone over too."

"Is that so?" I giggled, asking the bartender for water and a Passion Delight for Acaros.

"Yep," she said, sliding onto the stool in front of us. "Two guys actually."

"Two? I don't believe it."

"Bazzon and Varoth."

"Are those Acaros's friends?"

"Yep."

Another laugh bubbled up in my chest. "Did they run a train on you or something?"

"Sorry, my sex life is *private*," she said, throwing my words at me. "But yes."

"Mikayla, you can't say your sex life is private, then tell me about it." I grabbed my water from the bartender and sipped it. "Besides—"

Before I could get another word out of my mouth, someone yanked the water right out of my hand and threw it in my face. I shouted and jerked back in surprise, droplets pouring down my cheeks and onto my white top.

"Hey!" Mikayla shouted. "Get away from her!"

Through the wetness dripping from my lashes, I grabbed a napkin on the countertop and dapped the water off my face until I could see clearly. Acaros had practically flown over here and had Qina by the throat.

"What's going on?" I asked.

"I don't know, but this ends tonight. I'm going to find out who keeps sending this fucking bitch to fuck with you," he growled. He looked at the bartender. "Open a portal. I'm bringing her to The Chains."

"Portal's open," the bartender said.

While I would've had major insecurities with him leaving with her any other time, I found myself *wanting* her to be locked up in some demon prison so she couldn't bother me anymore. After last night, when Acaros had shown me how much he wanted me …

When he had fucked me in front of everyone …

When I had promised myself to him forever …

When he had brought me home, cleaned me, then dirtied me up again …

God, I wanted him to stay mine forever.

Heat coursed through my body to my core, and I tightened, desperate to clench around him, for this drama to be over, for me to be the only woman on Acaros's mind, and that couldn't happen until I was safe … and away from her.

"Go. I'll be fine here with them." I nodded to Bazzon and Varoth at our table.

"I don't trust them with you."

My eyes widened. "Why not? I thought that they were, like, your best friends."

"They're Lust demons," Acaros said. "You should never trust a Lust demon."

I crossed my arms. "Does that mean I shouldn't trust you?"

"No," he hissed. "I mean, you shouldn't trust a Lust demon with your girl."

Warmth spread through my body at the sound of this incubus calling me his girl. Again.

"Don't want to ruin the lovely conversation," Dani said, approaching us from a table. She placed her Passion Delight down on the counter and looped her arm around mine. "I'll keep an eye on her while you're gone."

Acaros arched a brow at her. "Last time, I found you in a Lust Room with her."

"After *you* let her through the portal," Dani argued. "Plus, I was showing her the palace."

After gritting his teeth, Acaros seized my hips and pulled me closer. "Your ass had better be here when I get back or else I will come find you," he murmured against my lips. "And you won't like the consequences."

Once I nodded *like a good girl*—as if I would actually follow all his orders—Acaros grabbed the back of Qina's neck and shoved her through the portal. Before stepping in after her, he peered back at me one last time.

When he completely disappeared, Dani tugged me toward the portal still swirling in the room that some demons used to leave this world so they could go back to their own. "We're not staying here. There's someplace better in Lust. Wanna go?"

"Better than here?"

"Way better," Mikayla said, shuffling off her seat. "Bazzon brought me there last night."

I arched a brow. "You've been to Hell?"

"To Lust," Mikayla corrected.

My gaze drifted to Jada, who was entranced by Professor Laufer, giggling and drinking Passion Delight like I had never seen before. Her hands were all over him, and his were on her body, between her legs, and—

Oh God.

Mikayla waved at them dismissively. "She'll be fine."

"I can see that," I hummed. "She's doing better than fine."

"So," Dani said, standing by the portal, "what do you say?"

"Will it make Acaros angry?" I asked.

"Probably." Dani giggled and looked over at her husband, or boyfriend ... I didn't know what to call the man who always seemed to hang around her. He didn't talk much to anyone else. She pulled me closer. "But angry incubi always fuck harder."

From what I had experienced so far, she wasn't wrong. Every time that I pissed Acaros off, he fucked me until I could barely walk, promising that he would breed me over and over and over again. And I couldn't get enough.

So, I took Dani's hand and stepped into the portal.

CHAPTER
TWENTY-EIGHT

ACAROS

"STATE YOUR BUSINESS," an icy-eyed demon guard said when I stepped out of the portal. He crossed his pale arms over his chest, his horns small and constructed of blue ice.

Through the window in the portal room, I watched snow drift from the sky outside.

Fucking hell, I hate the cold.

"I'm here to bring a prisoner to The Chains."

"I'm not a prisoner!" Qina screamed. "Let me go!"

She yanked her arms, tried biting and hitting me, even kicked me, but I didn't release my grip on her. Nobody enjoyed the Chains, and even I hated going there. But I was finished with this shit. She wasn't going to bother us again.

After a couple of moments, the guards stepped to the side and allowed us to pass through the door. As soon as I stepped outside, I winced at the chilling cold. The Kingdom of Pride wasn't hot, like everyone thought Hell to be.

It was ice.

Icicles dangled from white pine trees. Layers of snow lay atop a stone fence that stretched on for ten thousand miles. Two blue suns floated above the Pride ice castle, surrounded by glacier-like mountains on three sides.

"It's so fucking cold here," Qina hissed. "Let's go home."

"We don't have a home together," I growled, dragging her through the snow because I refused to take the cleared pathway. It took so much longer than cutting through the snow fields. And I didn't want to be with her another second.

Once we made it to a heavily guarded stone building, the guards opened the doors for us to enter. When the lights turned on, hundreds of demons rattled the iron cages that were stacked in the air and stuck their arms through the bars.

After I found an empty cage, I shoved Qina into it and clasped a silver chain around her flailing body, her neck, and her wrists. She screamed at the top of her lungs, body jerking everywhere and all at once.

"Stop!" she screamed. "It hurts."

"Tell me who fucking paid you off."

"Nobody!"

Instead of letting up like she begged me to do, I tightened my grip on the silver chain and let her skin melt off her body. Lust demons prided themselves on being pretty, but once silver burned her body, she'd never grow back as attractive as she was.

And she'd never been that attractive to begin with.

"Okay! Okay!" she shouted, snot rolling down her upper lip. "I'll tell you!"

As soon as the words left her mouth, I dropped one of the chains. It clattered against the floor and against her toes, burning off her toenail paint. She jumped back and hit the brick wall behind her, banging her head.

She's a fucking mess.

"Who the fuck sent you and Clayton?" I growled. "You get one more chance."

"I sent Clayton," she said.

I gritted my teeth, wanting nothing more than to strangle this woman to death with my own two hands and then suck out her soul so she would never be able to return to Earth or Hell.

"And who sent you?" I asked between my teeth.

"Isn't it obvious?"

My hand snapped around her throat, claws sinking into her flesh and tearing it apart. "If it was fucking obvious, then I wouldn't be in The Chains, wasting my time torturing you. I'd be back at my place, pounding Iza into the mattress with the problem already taken care of."

"You like her that much, huh?" Qina asked, clawing at my wrist.

I slammed her body as hard as I could into the wall, her head bouncing off the brick with a thud. When I pulled her away from it to do it again, blood stained the brown brick. Qina was nothing down here; not even royal blood could save her from what I would do to her.

When I slammed her again, she screamed out, "It's Dani!"

"What?" I asked.

"Dani sent me!" she exclaimed, arms and legs flailing. "Dani paid me to mess with Iza."

Hand slipping from around Qina's throat, I stepped back and shook my head. "Why?"

Qina landed on the ground, the skin on her knees tearing. "I don't know."

"Then, I don't believe you."

Dani was the queen of Lust and had been a human herself. She had absolutely no reason at all to mess with Iza, and I suspected that Qina just wanted me to kill Dani so it would be easier for her to steal her crown.

Not that Eros would ever let that happen.

"I'm not lying," she said, crawling toward me. "Believe me."

"No."

"I'm telling you the truth. She paid me to mess with her." Qina shrugged her shoulders. "I don't know the exact reasons, but she mentioned something about the war with the angels that's approaching. That she could use Iza."

"Why would she need to use Iza?" I asked.

The mischief faded from Qina's eyes, and suddenly, they were a crystal-clear green color, that of Envy. Qina wasn't acting off any feelings of desire or lust for me. Her jealousy over Iza was shining through, and it wasn't because Iza had me.

No, it was because Iza had power. And Envy demons always sought power.

"She's special," Qina whispered. "And you practically gave her right to Dani."

CHAPTER
TWENTY-NINE

IZA

"WHERE ARE YOU BRINGING ME?" I asked Dani because we didn't step out into Lust.

The dry air of the portal room slithered around my throat, like a serpent did to its prey. I coughed and walked down the blackened steps to the large, unguarded orange doors. When Dani pushed open the doors, I stepped into an even more suffocating arena.

"Welcome to Wrath," she said.

Wilted leaves hung off the brittle trees, falling away with the humid breeze. Large steel gates glimmered underneath the orange sun in the distance. Fires burned in every direction as ash rained from the sky.

Dani took my hand. "You're safe here. I'm dating the son of Satan."

"But I thought you were married to that other demon."

"Eros?" she asked with a giggle. "I am."

"And you're dating someone else too?" I asked.

"A few people actually ..." She guided me down a long path filled with horrid screams from people I couldn't see. Children with sharp red horns and vexed stares ran by us on the busy cobblestone walkway and made a beeline for the gates. "Biast, Minseok, Luficer."

My eyes nearly popped out of my head. "Lucifer? Like, the Lucifer?"

She smirked. "The Devil himself."

A small giggle left my lips. "So, do you like … tell him what to do since you're the leader?"

"Oh boy, I wish," she said. "He leads the Kingdom of Pride. There are many realms here—Lust, Pride, Wrath, Greed, Envy, Gluttony, Sloth, and even some smaller ones in between that house many different races, like humans, demons, werewolves, and vampires."

"Wow," I whispered. "I didn't know humans lived here."

"I'll have to take you to Durnbone sometime," she said with a smile. "One of the demon kings in Durnbone is mated to a human. I think you both could get along quite well, and I'm sure Maxine would love to meet you."

"That would be great," I whispered.

Maybe she could give me some pointers about dating a demon.

Instead of going through the gates and into the kingdom, Dani led me down an arid path near the gate entrance toward rivers of lava. Bones drifted down the river, brittle and fleshless. I held my breath at the stench.

"What are we doing here?" I asked Dani as we stopped feet from the lava.

"I want you to meet someone."

"Who?"

"A fallen angel."

A tall, angry demon emerged from the river, lava dripping down his body. "Dani."

"Biast," Dani exclaimed. "This is Iza. Iza, Biast."

After barely sparing me a glance, he nodded to the other side of the river. "He's here."

Dani wrapped one arm around Biast's arm and the other around mine, pulling me toward the river of literally flesh-melting lava. I dug my heels into the ground in an attempt to stop her from moving me.

"Come on," she said. "You won't get hurt."

"It's lava."

"I've gone in this river a million times."

"You're a demon!" I exclaimed. "I'm not."

"You won't burn," Biast said. "Keep hold of Dani."

Dani yanked me closer, and I tried to stumble back. But before I could, she had tugged me all the way in. I winced and waited for the searing pain to begin melting me alive, but all the lava felt like was warm sea water.

My feet reached the bottom of the river, and I walked with Dani and Biast to the other side. Chest rising and falling quickly because I hadn't expected to survive a river of lava, I shook the excess lava off my body like a wet dog.

"We are at war," Dani said.

"With who?" I asked, looking back as Dani led us deeper into the brittle woods.

"The angels and God herself."

"Herself?"

"Yes, unlike what the Church believes, God is a woman."

A couple of moments later, we emerged from the brittle forest and stepped out into a clearing, where a man sat, naked and chained up to a tree.

"This is Minseok," Dani said.

"Why is he in chains?" I asked. "I thought you said he was your lover?"

"It's ... complicated." Dani sighed softly. "He's a recently fallen angel."

"I'm not a fallen angel. *You* sank your claws into me and pulled me down. I am here against my will." Minseok yanked on the chains that burned into his body. His wings were completely bare. When he looked at me, his eyes widened. "Beliel ..."

"Who's Beliel?" I asked Dani.

"Beliel was the first fallen angel who prophesied about the war I mentioned earlier," Dani said, reciting the prophecy. *"Three demons will rise from the ashes—the Devil, the Beast, the False Prophet. God will call them the Triad of Sinners; we will call them the Unholy Trinity. Under them, Hell will rule the Earth, and heaven will fall to ruin."*

My eyes widened slightly, and I looked back at Minseok, who still stared at me in disbelief. I furrowed my brows and averted my gaze, not liking the way he looked at me like he knew something that I didn't.

Dani fished into her pocket and pulled out her vibrating phone. "Give me a second."

After I nodded, she tapped a button on her phone, took Biast's hand, and walked deeper into the forest.

How did phones even work down here? Were there cell towers and satellites that connected with Earth?

"You need to get out of here," Minseok said. "Now."

My eyes widened, and I glanced over at him. "Why?"

"Because they're using you."

"For what?"

A branch snapped behind me, and I twisted my head, expecting to see Dani.

But instead, a demon who looked similar to Biast with red skin and a huge body that towered over me stood at the trees. "What's a human doing in these parts? Come to play?"

"Get out of here," Minseok shouted. "Now!"

I shuffled backward, my arms suddenly feeling so heavy and tingly. "What's going on?"

Before I could mutter another word, the demon lunged at me. I didn't remember what happened next, just that my tingling arms burned with such an intensity that I thought I was still in the river. And then the demon's neck snapped, everything suddenly went black, and I heard Acaros's voice drifting through my ears.

CHAPTER
THIRTY

ACAROS

A DEMON CORPSE lay at my feet. I shuffled back a few feet, yet some kind of power emanating from Iza's body wrapped around both my ankles like snakes and dragged me toward her, my body feeling like it was being crushed from the inside out.

Everything happened so quickly that I didn't know how to stop it. One moment, I had been hunting Iza down and following her scent into Wrath; the next moment, I'd watched her kill a demon in a split second.

She tightened her grip on me. "Acaros! Help me! I can't see anything."

"Release your hold on me, Iza."

"I-I don't know how!" she exclaimed. "I don't know what's happening."

I had been in war and battle, and usually, demons went for the souls, to suck them right out of the body and end a demon's life for good if they were trying to kill another. Typically, I could fight back. But I couldn't. Not this time.

When Iza pulled me all the way to her, her eyes were pure white with a ring of black around the edges. With the last of my energy, I reached out and grabbed her hand. Iza took a huge breath and stumbled back, releasing the magic.

She landed on her ass and stared at the corpse a couple of feet away.

"Oh my God," Iza whispered. "Oh my God. Oh my God. Oh my God!"

After shaking her head, she slowly backed away from the demon's corpse. Usually, a demon couldn't die unless another demon—or angel—sucked out their soul and stored it in their own. But I couldn't even see a remnant of a soul.

None.

Not even a smidgen of mist anywhere.

Which meant that this demon's soul was still intact in his body, but he was dead.

"Impossible," I whispered.

Iza turned to me with heavy tears in her wavering eyes. "Acaros, wh-what did I do?" She ran toward me, hands shaking. "I didn't mean it. Is he dead? I-I don't even know what h-h-happened."

"It's okay, Iza," I said, still staring at the demon.

Nobody had this kind of power. Nobody alive at least.

A tree branch snapped to my left, and I glanced over to see Dani emerging from the dead trees.

She set her gaze on the man, then looked at Iza, her lips turning into a small smile. "I knew it."

"What is going on?!" I exclaimed, wrapping one arm around Iza's shoulders and pulling her toward me. I shifted my body to shield Iza from Dani, in case Dani had put some kind of spell on her. "What have you done?"

"I didn't do anything," Dani said.

"You heard me tell Iza to stay at The Lounge," I growled. "And you brought her *here*?!"

"I needed to make sure."

"Make sure of what?!"

Dani pursed her lips together. "That she was the one."

Iza trembled in fear beside me, her body shivering in panic. I tucked her into the crook of my arm and held her even tighter in an attempt to calm her down while I took care of Dani, the queen of Lust and apparently now an enemy.

"What the fuck are you talking about?" I snarled.

"Do you know Beliel's Prophecy?" Dani asked me.

"*Three demons will rise from the ashes—the Devil, the Beast, the False Prophet. God will call them the Triad of Sinners; we will call them the Unholy Trinity. Under them, Hell will rule the Earth, and heaven will fall to ruin,*" I repeated from memory.

As demon boys and girls, we had been forced to memorize the prophecy, had been told that it would be fulfilled soon. But *soon* in demon years could be hundreds or thousands of years from now.

What did that have to do with this?

"What you learned, what Eros learned, and what your friends learned wasn't the entirety of the prophecy. Pieces of it had been sheltered away, hidden within each of the seven kingdoms. And we found another piece two months ago, just days after the war began."

"Where did you find it?"

"The Kingdom of Wrath."

"And what'd it say?"

"Written on the walls of the Tartarus Caves, it reads: *Twenty-three years before the war begins, a human will be born who possesses the same image of who angels call Mother—hair set in pretty coils, dark skin that glows in the sunset, and innocent brown eyes so everyone thinks she can do no harm. And with her, my power will lie.*"

Eyes widening slightly, I shifted my gaze to Iza. "*God* looks like Iza?"

"Yes," Dani said. "I've spoken with her."

"And you think that Iza has Beliel's powers?"

"I've thought that since I met her." Dani gestured for us to walk to the lava pits that demons had to trek through to even get here. "If she didn't, there isn't a way that she would survive multiple nights with any Lust demon. Especially you."

"Why didn't you tell me this sooner?" I asked, picking Iza up and following Dani.

"Because"—she smiled softly—"I haven't known you for long, but it was the first time I had seen you so happy. I wasn't going to ruin that before I knew if Iza certainly possessed the powers of Beliel. Besides, Eros told me not to get involved."

Iza stirred in my arms, still shaking.

After turning her attention to Iza, she nodded. "So, will you join us?"

"No," I said.

"I'm not asking you," Dani said to me. "I'm asking Iza."

I growled. "I don't care who you're asking."

"Iza is perfectly capable of making her own decisions."

"Decisions about a war that she knows nothing about? Decisions based on her power that she just realized today—that she also knows little about?" I pulled her tighter. "She's not making any hasty decisions based on a prophecy that we don't even know to be true."

"The prophecy is true," Dani said. "Ask any of the commanders. And the war is here."

"She doesn't—" I started, only for Dani to interrupt me.

"I don't expect that we'll need Iza anytime soon," Dani said. "It'll give you and others a chance to train her to become stronger. She has the power of all the kingdoms, not just Lust. So, she will need extensive training."

"What if I don't want this?" Iza asked softly, her voice barely audible. Her eyes kept opening and closing in a haze.

"Then, don't accept," Dani said, offering another smile. "But please take your time and think about it."

CHAPTER
THIRTY-ONE

IZA

WITH MY GAZE on Acaros's ceiling, I blew out a low breath in an attempt to relieve the stress from last week. I willingly hadn't left the Kingdom of Lust—not even for class—because I now had way more important things to worry about than Advanced Statistics and Literature.

I had powers …

Powers that I couldn't quite understand. Powers that continued to fester inside me, the more and more that I stayed in Lust. And in all my years of living in the real world, nothing felt as good as this.

After turning onto my side, I pushed some hair out of Acaros's face. He was in his human form—a weird sight down in Lust—and he hadn't had a haircut probably since the day I'd met him. It was growing out, almost shaggy on his forehead.

My lips curled into a small smile, and I cuddled closer to him. Another reason why I hadn't left Lust was because of this man, who had tied me to the bed nearly every night and pounded into me, vowing to get me pregnant so I *couldn't* help Dani.

Turned out that his parents—one fully from the Kingdom of Wrath, which was where he had gotten his red demon skin from, and one half Lust, half Envy—had been killed by Dani during her ascension as queen. Acaros hadn't had hard feelings against her—at least from what I was aware—until she took me.

Once I placed a kiss on his cheek, I slipped out of bed and walked to the bathroom. I might not have left, but that didn't mean Jada and Mikayla hadn't come over and brought some much-needed human food and goods to me.

One of those goods being ... *this*.

I shut the bathroom door behind me, reached to the back of the closet where I had hidden the box, and pulled out a box of pregnancy tests. After deciding that it wouldn't turn out positive—because, I mean, didn't demons have dead sperm like vampires? Wasn't that how it worked?—I peed on one for the joke of it.

While I was mid-pee, Acaros banged on the door. "Are you okay?"

My eyes widened, and I hurried to finish up before he could barge into the room. "Fine!"

"Jada and Mikayla are here," he called.

"Already?!" I cried. "What time is it?"

"Apparently, ten on Earth."

Time worked a bit differently here, and I was slowly getting used to the change.

So, once I placed the test down on the counter and washed my hands, I shuffled out of the bathroom and down the steps. Acaros opened the front door, letting in my friends.

Mikayla whizzed by us, running up to the bathroom and holding her legs together. "Sorry! I have to pee so badly! That portal always scares the piss out of me!"

Jada walked into the living room as Acaros stepped outside with Bazzon, Varoth, and Professor Laufer, who had all come along. We were supposed to have a picnic in the Garden of Passion today to celebrate. I didn't know *what* we were celebrating, but Mikayla had said to wear a party hat.

Not that I had one ...

"Biiiiiiitttttcccchh!" Mikayla called from the bathroom. "I know this isn't what I think it is!"

I furrowed my brows and glanced over at Jada, who shrugged. "You know how crazy s—"

Before Jada could finish her sentence, Mikayla ran out of the bathroom, holding my pregnancy stick in the air and waving it around like a maniac. Thank God that Acaros and his buddies were outside because I would've died on the spot.

"It says positive!" Mikayla screamed.

"Mikayla, can you please shut—"

The door behind us slammed open, and Acaros peered into the room. "What's positive?"

While I tried to peel the stick away from Mikayla before he could see it, it fell out of her grasp and right at the feet of Acaros. He peered down at it quizzically, as if he had never seen a pregnancy test before, and picked it up.

Heart pounding inside my chest, I fiddled with my fingers behind my back and shuffled in front of Acaros. I knew he would be thrilled, but I was still so nervous because ... I'd never thought that this would happen so soon.

Not only so soon since I'd met him, but so soon in my life.

Acaros's confused expression softened, and he looked down at me. "Is this ..."

"Yes!" Mikayla screeched.

Jada elbowed her hard in the ribs, then grabbed her hand and yanked her out the front door to give us some privacy. "Come on."

When the door closed, I swallowed hard and walked closer to him, grabbing his hands. "I'm scared," I whispered. I didn't even know what kind of human-demon hybrid would come out of my vagina in nine months. "I didn't think it would happen so soon. What about Dani?"

Acaros set the test down on the arm of the couch, then cupped my face with his hands. He drew the pads of his thumbs across my cheekbones, a small smile crossing his face. "Hellcat, I'm so fucking excited."

I slapped him across his chest, making him let out a low chuckle. "Acaros!"

"I'll still train you to become stronger," he murmured, drawing my face closer to his. "And after you give birth in a few months, if you still want to work with Dani ... then I won't stop you. I'll be a— what do you call it on Earth? A stay-at-home dad."

"A few months?!" I exclaimed. "What do you mean, a few months?"

"Demons are only typically pregnant for a few months."

I arched a brow. "So, you're telling me that I don't have nine months to prepare?!"

"Nine months? What the fuck? That's such a long time."

After crossing my arms over my chest, I stared up at him, trying to look menacing that he had put this demon baby inside me and that I only had a few months to prepare to bring another life into this world, but honestly ... the thought of Acaros becoming even softer with it did something to me.

Imagining him being a stay-at-home dad?! Butterflies filled my chest.

I mean, that couldn't be so bad, could it?

Maybe this whole thing would work out just the way it was supposed to in the end.

CHAPTER
THIRTY-TWO

IZA

FOUR WEEKS and a very pregnant belly later, I stepped through the portal into an unfamiliar icy kingdom. Usually, Acaros didn't let me go anywhere alone, but while he was out, I had snuck away to have a chat with Qina and to find Clayton.

My breath mingled with the frigid air, creating a cloud of white in front of my face. I made some excuse to the guards standing at attention in the portal room and found my way onto the stone walkways.

The chill seeped into my bones, and yet the power within me began to stir. Even with all the training Acaros had put me through the past few weeks, I hadn't been able to control it, at least not to the extent that I needed to control it for Dani.

Though ... I wasn't sure if I wanted to be part of this war.

I thought it would take hours to find the prison in the Kingdom of Pride that Dani had mentioned Clayton and Qina were in, but it only took about twenty minutes of waddling like a penguin. A towering and heavily guarded building lay ahead, its iron gates covered in ice.

The guards stationed at the entrance peered at me with

narrowed eyes, their expressions cold and indifferent. Cradling my belly bump and trying to look like a helpless woman, I walked up to them and gave a small smile.

"What business do you have here?" one guard asked, tone strong.

"I'm here to release prisoners of Lust."

The guards exchanged a brief glance. "State your name and title."

"I'm Iza."

"And title?" another guard repeated.

I opened my mouth a handful of times, not sure of what I should say. Not many people knew that I had the power of Beliel inside me, and I believed that Dani wanted to keep it that way. It was a hidden power that—if I decided to use—would help us.

As tension began to mount, a smooth voice drifted through the air from behind the guards, and I noticed that one of the entry doors had been opened. "Do be kind to our guest, gentlemen. She's braved quite the journey. I've been expecting her."

With white hair and eyes of pure ice, a demon stepped from behind the guards. Wind seemed to whip around his large blue horns, and even the guards seemed *intimidated* by his presence.

He reached out a hand. "Lucifer."

"Lucifer," I repeated, mouth dry. "You're Lucifer?"

"The one and only." His lips curved into a smirk. "Usually, humans like you cower at the mere mention of my name."

"Have you been to Earth lately?" I asked, the powers within me stirring and giving me confidence that I once hadn't had. "Everyone jokes about going to Hell. Your name is only feared by the true believers of God, and there aren't many of them anymore."

"That's thanks to you, *old friend*," he hummed.

I shared a long look with him because I was no *old friend* of Lucifer. But Dani had mentioned that Beliel had corrupted Lucifer when they were still in Heaven. Dani hadn't been there either, but Lucifer was apparently still connected to her.

And if he was connected to her, then he would recognize her.

He would recognize *me*.

His eyes glistened with amusement as I realized that he understood who I was. He intertwined his fingers and tilted his chin slightly upward, the smirk widening even more. "I would say that I have missed you, but I've been enjoying my time down here."

After humming softly because I didn't have any memory of Beliel—only her power—I rocked back on my heels. "I would like entrance into The Chains to release two prisoners of Lust. I'm here not on anyone's orders, but my own."

A low chuckle left his mouth. "Does Dani know this?"

"No."

"Your ... husband? Boyfriend? What is that guy to you again?"

"Acaros," I stated, "is my fiancé." *Sorta.* "But, no, he doesn't know."

"They just let you roam around by yourself?"

"They don't own me. I make my own decisions."

"Spoken like your true self." Another laugh left his mouth, and he stepped to the side to allow me entrance. "Go ahead. Release the prisoners of Lust." As I walked past him, he snatched my elbow and leaned in closer. "But I will be seeing you around, Beliel."

CHAPTER
THIRTY-THREE

IZA

THE SCENT of shit drifted through my nose. I gagged and held my breath, stepping into the brightly lit prison. Cages were stacked on top of each other to the ceiling and all throughout the building.

I pressed my lips together, trying not to let these hissing demons intimidate me, and walked through the cages to search for Clayton first. I didn't care so much about Qina, but I thought it was wrong to keep her locked up here for so long when *Dani* had been the one to send them both my way.

Acaros had other thoughts, but I didn't care. He had been acting off possessiveness and jealousy when he put Clayton down here. And I wasn't about to let that poor, nerdy boy suffer any longer.

"Iza," Clayton shouted to my left, clanging on the metal bars. "What are you—"

After whipping my head around to spot him, I ran over to him. He knelt in the cage, dark bags underneath his eyes. I searched my pocket for a key that I might or might not have stolen off Lucifer when he grabbed me by the elbow. Once I shoved it into the lock, I yanked the door open, my fingers burning as they touched the metal.

"Sorry that it took me so long to come and get you," I said. *I honestly forgot.*

"Does Acaros know that—"

"No."

Instead of following me farther down the walkway of cages, he inched back toward his own and lingered near the door. "Yeah, then ... I'm just going to stay here. I don't want him killing me when he finds out that—"

"That boy is not going to kill you," I said, hand running over my belly. "He's soft now that we have her on the way."

Clayton dropped his gaze down to my belly, then widened his eyes. "You're pregnant?"

"Yes. Now, help me find Qina, so we can get out of this bitter cold."

A couple of moments passed, and Clayton still stood at the cage door, as if contemplating whether or not he should actually follow me. But after a second, he nodded and headed my way, extending his arm toward a couple of chains on the right. "She's over here."

When we made it to her cell, Qina was passed out in the back, her once-smooth-and-soft skin now wrinkled and her hair graying. My eyes widened as I wondered how she could've transformed like *this* in only a couple of weeks. Yet she was still beautiful.

"Qina?" I asked.

Qina blinked her eyes open and sat up, brows furrowed. "What's going on?"

"We're releasing you," I said, plunging the key into the lock and swinging open the door. I crouched in front of it to get a better look inside and gave her my most pointed stare. "But if you even think about laying a hand on or flirting with Acaros, I will throw you in here myself."

Sitting up a bit taller, Qina grasped her head and nodded, her features returning youthful. "I only flirt with men for money. Not for enjoyment." She peered up at me, then held her hands up in defense. "But Acaros is off-limits."

"Good," I said, stepping to the side so she could escape the cage.

We walked down the cages and out the prison exit, into the biting cold. Wind seared my cheeks, and I slouched down in my hoodie to protect my ears, which felt like they were freezing the hell off.

I need to get home!

"Why'd you let me out anyway?" Qina asked.

"Because she's nice," Clayton said. "You should appreciate it."

Qina scrunched her nose. "Still have a hard-on for her? Wait until Acaros hears that."

Clayton covered his groin. "I do not have a hard-on for her."

"Mmhmm," Qina hummed.

Clayton's ears reddened. "I don't, Qina."

My lips curled into a small smile. *They'd be cute together.*

"Sure, let's call it—"

Before Qina could finish her sentence, the white sky broke for a moment, and a blinding light blasted through the air, knocking us back. I landed on my side and cradled my belly, hoping our baby wasn't hurt.

In front of us, a woman emerged from the sky, the feathers on her white wings burning off, the dust floating in the breeze. Her bare wings cracked and crumbled to pieces, and she landed on the ground, feet from us.

Within a moment, Clayton was on his feet, shielding me from her. "Who are—"

"You are abominations," she whispered, her voice cold and commanding. With one flick of a finger, she sent Clayton through the air and a quarter mile south. She stepped closer to us. "We will purge this entire world."

With a swift motion, the angel struck a bolt of light through Qina, sending her back, even farther than Clayton. The crash echoed through the frozen kingdom, and I stood, the ground trembling underneath my feet.

For a moment, I prepared myself for her rumbling attack. But she peered at me in confusion, and then a burst of energy rushed through my body. My vision darkened so I couldn't see the world around me, but the angel's aura glowed a deep red.

The aura lifted into the air. Twisted in ways that it shouldn't. Limbs were ripped off and thrown around the kingdom. And then the gooey sound of guts dripping onto a stone walkway drifted through my ears.

I blinked a few times, my vision slowly coming back to me, enough so I could spot the angel lying on the pavement, dead, all her limbs broken off and her body twisted in several directions. I sucked in a sharp breath and steadied my woozy body.

And it was in that moment when I made up my mind. I didn't care what anyone thought or said ... I needed to be in this war.

CHAPTER
THIRTY-FOUR

ACAROS

THE FLUORESCENT LIGHTS inside Target cast a glow on the aisle of baby clothes. I pushed the cart toward the small dresses that weren't bigger than the size of my palm and stopped in front of a pink dress with flowers and a matching bow.

My lips curled into a small smile, warmth spreading through me.

I picked it off the rack and placed it into my carriage with the fifteen other outfits I had chosen today. Iza had snuck off somewhere this morning—probably to see Dani or her friends—and I had all today to myself …

Just to browse the baby section of all the human stores.

An array of tiny onesies and miniature dresses lined the aisles. I ran my claws over the soft fabrics, my heart pounding faster than it ever had at the thought of bringing a hellion into this world soon. How would she look?

Like Iza or me? Maybe a mix of both with dark brown skin and small red horns.

After biting back the chuckle that rose through my chest and up my throat, I took another outfit from the aisle and headed toward the toys section. If I came home with our daughter's entire wardrobe and Iza hadn't gotten to pick any of it, I assumed she'd be angry.

Before I left the aisle, I stopped and grabbed one more outfit because Iza wouldn't be angry if we had a cute demon baby crawling around in one-piece suits, adorned with stars and flowers and animal designs, right?

I mean, *how* could she be mad at that?

Once I exited the aisle, I swung around the women's section, which was on the way to the toys, and searched for any matching outfits that I could get Iza. Butterflies fluttered inside my chest, and I realized how soft I had become in just a couple of weeks.

But I didn't mind much, especially if I could find matching outfits for them.

Yet with the warmth that filled my chest also lay uncertainty. The clothes were so small, and they would fit an even smaller baby. A baby that we'd have to protect, not only from the cruel world, but also from the angels above.

War was coming whether we wanted it or not.

Once I picked out a couple of toys—*I need to save some shopping for Iza*—I checked out my items at the counter. As I left the store with the garments neatly packed in two bags, I headed toward my car.

My phone buzzed in my pocket, but with the bags in both my arms, I let it ring until it stopped buzzing. But a moment later, it rang again. I set the bags on the top of the car and pulled my phone out of my pocket, spotting Iza's number.

"Hellcat, wait until you see all the outfits that I bought—" I answered.

"Acaros, I need to talk to you," Iza said, voice full of concern. "It's important."

My claws lengthened. "What is it? What happened?"

There was a long silence on the other end of the phone.

"Iza, what the fuck happened?" I growled, throwing the bags into the back seat and slipping into the driver's seat so I could get somewhere private to open a portal to Hell and find Iza now. "Where are you?"

She sniffled. "I … I killed her."

My heart dropped, and for a moment, I thought she was talking about our daughter.

"Who?" I asked, heart pounding.

"I … I don't know," she whispered. "Please don't be mad."

"I'm not mad, but tell me where you are."

"I'm in Pride with Clayton and Qina. I let them out because they'd been trapped in that prison for weeks now and I felt bad. And on our way back …" She sniffled again as a couple of people chatted in the background.

"Fucking Qina," I growled, stepping on the gas and driving toward The Lounge, where I could quickly and easily set up a portal to Pride. "If she touched you, I will suck her soul from her body and—"

"She didn't touch me," Iza said. "An angel fell from the sky above … and attacked us."

I skidded to a stop in the alleyway behind The Lounge and sprinted out of the car to the club. After shoving open the door, I immediately opened a portal and stepped through it, rushing toward Pride as quickly as I could.

The line crackled and suddenly went silent.

Curse the bad cell service in these fucking portals!

When I stepped out into Pride, a chilling wind whipped around me. I bit my tongue at how fucking cold it was here and pushed past the guards in the portal room, heading down the stone path and following fresh footprints.

"Iza!" I called out, the wind carrying my voice.

I continued to run until I spotted a group of demons gathered in a field, Lucifer and Iza among them. When Iza saw me, she hurried my way and buried her face into the center of my chest, her chin quivering.

"I'm sorry," she mumbled. "I-I don't like killing."

Wrapping my arms around her shoulders, I pulled her toward

me and assessed the situation. Body parts lay all over the place, and the torso of the fallen angel seemed to be twisted in many directions.

Clayton and Qina were being checked out by some medics, but looked badly bruised.

Iza placed her chin on the center of my chest and stared up at me through teary eyes. "I don't like killing, but she came down here and tossed Clayton and Qina around like they were nothing. And I know you don't like them, but it was unjustified. If this is how the rest of the war will be, then ... I want to be part of it."

I swallowed and dropped one of my hands to her belly bump. "Not until you give birth."

"Not until I give birth," she repeated. "But if I have the power to help you and our family, then I will. I'm done being a pushover. I'm strong, and I want to start being strong. I want our daughter to know that her parents are powerful and protective of not only her, but of our kind too." Something sparkled in her eyes. "I want to win this war."

I snatched up her hand and squeezed. "Then, we will win."

Continue reading in the epilogue!

ALSO BY EMILIA ROSE

ABOUT THE AUTHOR

Emilia Rose is a USA Today bestselling author of steamy romance. She loves writing about dirty-talking bad boys who are obsessed with innocent, and sometimes insecure, virgin heroines. She currently lives in a small town in Connecticut USA with her husband and three playful cats.

Join Emilia's newsletter for exclusive giveaways, early chapter releases, and more!

Made in the USA
Middletown, DE
29 August 2024